I0738144

RAGING RIVER

HAROLD DAWKINS

RAGING RIVER

DJR PUBLISHING

Fayetteville, Tennessee

Copyright © 2023 Harold Dawkins

All rights reserved. No part or any portion of this book may be reproduced in any form, mechanical, digital, or transmitted without the author's prior written permission, except for the use of brief quotations in a book review.

This novel is a work of fiction. Names, characters, places, and incidents are the product of the author's imagination and do not depict real persons or events. Any resemblance to actual people or incidents is entirely coincidental.

For information about this title or to order other books and/or electronic media, contact the publisher:

DJR Publishing
925 Greenview Drive
Fayetteville, TN 37334

Cover and interior design by The Book Cover Whisperer:
OpenBookDesign.biz

978-0-578-36986-0 Paperback
978-0-578-36987-7 eBook

Printed in the United States of America

FIRST EDITION

RAGING RIVER

PREFACE

⊹

THIS FICTIONAL STORY IS BASED ON A SPECIFIC HISTORICAL timeline; however, the references to Petersburg, as well as other towns in the region, have been described with liberal imagination by the author. Petersburg was in serious decline by the late 1830s and only claimed to be populated by three families in 1854. Therefore, the book does not fit the true definition of historical fiction based on the placement of Petersburg as a declining but still viable community in 1898. My hope is that the true historians from the region will be able to accept my slightly embellished timeline in order to suit my chosen time period for this story which attempts to portray the years in which my grandfather owned and operated Chamberlain's Ferry.

I have always been interested in the history of Petersburg, Georgia. According to historical records, it was the third-largest city in the state in the early 1800s. Like several small communities near the Savannah River in Lincoln County, Georgia, Petersburg was covered by water soon after the construction of a dam. Evidence of the city's building foundations can be seen during times of extremely low lake levels.

—

MY GREAT-GRANDFATHER, LOUIS NAPOLEON Chamberlain, died twenty years to the day before I was born. Chamberlain's Ferry provided passage across the Savannah River between McCormick and Lincoln counties. His family homeplace was located off Chamberlain Ferry Road in McCormick, South Carolina. I have pictures of the house taken when it was still standing on the property. A few years ago, my brother, Steven, and I walked the premises where the only remaining evidence of the homeplace is the low concrete wall that surrounded the house.

HIS DAUGHTER, KATE CHAMBERLAIN Leverett, was my grandmother. The Petersburg boarding house referred to in the book was my attempt to describe Grandma Kate's home that was located behind Lincolnton United Methodist Church in Lincolnton, Georgia for many years. That two-story home was moved out in the county years ago when the church purchased the property following the passing of my grandmother. The church expanded its facilities by building a fellowship hall on the lot in the same place where the house once stood. The house is now located off Highway 220 not far from its intersection with the Augusta Highway. The Lincoln Journal reported that the home was once "a very popular boarding house for local schoolteachers."

I remember attending the Methodist church with my grandmother when I was young, and she was still able to walk the short distance down the sidewalk to the church. To this day, I credit her for instilling in me at a young age the importance of going to church.

A few miles up Chamberlain's Ferry Road on the Georgia side, in Lincoln County, you will find an old brick store that was operated by Uncle Albert and Aunt Sudie Chamberlain Sims. Aunt Sudie, as we called her, was my grandmothers' sister.

ACKNOWLEDGMENT

I WOULD LIKE TO THANK MY WIFE, LEE ANN, FOR HER constant support. She has always served as my most enthusiastic cheerleader. Her skill as an editor, from her many years of teaching children to write in our public school systems, has proven invaluable. She spent months poring over my words and sentences making suggestions and improvements.

I am appreciative of the writings by Steve Luking and Dwain Moss about Chamberlain's Ferry which were instrumental in the formation of this story. Much of my inspiration came from their stories and pictures, as well as my own memories about my Chamberlain/Leverett family roots.

I would also like to thank my family, and friends who encouraged me by providing the memories, stories, and the inspiration that made this novel possible. I especially want to thank my good friend and avid reader Gary. Gary was the first person I entrusted to read the full manuscript.

His encouraging words made me feel like a "New York Best Selling Author" even though I may never achieve that honor. Lynn, my sister-in-law, also provided much-appreciated insight.

Chapter 1

Parksville, SC, 1898

As the July sun reached its peak, Robert's brow beaded with sweat from the strain of leading the mule in a near-straight row. Planting tobacco was hard work, he was used to that, but it was the voices in his head that distracted him with each step. "Never again," he whispered through clenched teeth. The pain of yet another broken relationship was so difficult that it caused him to doubt he would ever be able to find a loving, trustworthy partner. He had already reconciled himself to the idea of spending the rest of his life as a bachelor. At least that way he felt sure he would never again be hurt by falling in love with the wrong person. Robert pondered how he had become emotionally entangled with a woman who clearly valued her own needs above his.

He paused, rubbed the back of his neck, and breathed a heavy sigh. The day was bright and cloudless, and summer humidity hung in the air like a dense fog, stealing his breath. Freshly plowed soil seemed closer to the consistency of clay than dirt as it was turned up with each movement of the blade. The red bandana tied around Robert's neck was wet and dark. His brown boots were now discolored and so heavy from the caked-on red clay that they felt twenty pounds heavier than normal. His blue overalls were dirty and stained from the knee down. Blonde hair curled on his forehead from underneath the bandana, and each strand seemed to contain a drop of moisture perched to overcome its own weight and plummet to the ground. His arm and leg muscles strained to force the plow deeper and further into the packed earth with each forward surge. Robert's throat was parched and burning. His shadow cast a long image on the ground. Yet another day was slowly fading away.

The work was demanding and physically stressful, but Robert did not normally complain. It was customary in Parksville, South Carolina, for the oldest male siblings to put work ahead of education or relationships. At the age of twenty-four, the responsibility of helping provide for his family was at times a great burden. The Chamber's farm was not large compared to many tobacco growers in the area, but it was large enough to provide for their needs, harvesting a little less than one thousand pounds of tobacco per year. The farm was located east of the railroad tracks that passed through Parksville, with the Savannah River two miles to the west. In addition to the tobacco fields, they also owned cows, pigs, horses, chickens, and one mule.

Robert's grandfather, Elijah Chambers, at thirty, had laid claim to six hundred acres in an 1804 land grant which later he willed to his children. Elijah and Anne Chambers migrated from Virginia to North Carolina, along with other pioneers seeking inexpensive land, finally settling in South Carolina. Elijah taught his sons how to grow tobacco just as Robert's father, William Chambers, had taught him. At the time of Robert's grandfather's death, William inherited a portion of the estate along with a brother, a sister, and a sister-in-law. Each received the same apportionment of land.

William's older brother died fighting with Confederate forces at the Battle of Chickamauga. His widow and only son received some furniture, and a pony from the estate, along with his older brother's portion of land which they immediately sold to William. Following the death of her husband, she remarried in less than three months to a man from her church. Robert's parents seemed to always avoid talking about William's sister-in-law as though there was something about her that they didn't want anyone to know. She and her new husband shortly after moved to Columbia, South Carolina, and never visited again. William's younger brother lost his land to foreclosure within three years of receiving it from the estate. His sister and her husband were not farmers and never really had any interest in the land. Her husband had grown up in more modern large cities so after a few years they sold their land and moved away. They would occasionally visit, but Robert had not seen any of them now in over a year.

Robert dreamed of a life far removed from this backbreaking labor that for now offered few rewards. Daydreaming became a valuable pastime for him while working. At least it kept his mind from the disturbing thoughts, which at times seemed to spin endlessly in his head. Despite the heartache, he still held on to the belief that real love was attainable and that once he found it, his life would be changed for the better.

Robert struggled to believe that this had been his life now for the past five years. Where had the time gone? The grind of daily chores before and after school had somewhat melted the last few years together forming a repeating and predictable pattern that didn't allow for much of a personal life. Farming seemed to be all he knew now. Sunday was the only day that his father agreed to take on his chores allowing him some freedom. The family no longer attended church because of the recent challenging growing seasons which required their constant attention on the farm.

A recent drought had made this year's tobacco crop a challenging one. Leaves now hung in the curing barn while the fields were already being prepared for the next crop. Tobacco had been the cash crop for the Broad River Valley for years, but more recently many farmers were converting their fields to grow cotton. Robert and his father were familiar with tobacco. They knew what to expect from their crops and were hesitant to join other farmers who had made the transition from tobacco to cotton. Still, tobacco remained the predominant crop. Longboats loaded with hogsheads of tobacco could be seen daily being steered by an oarsman who navigated the river to reach markets in Augusta.

Robert looked up and chuckled to himself seeing his sister Susie crossing the field. She was straining as though she were carrying the weight of a pack mule instead of a bucket of water. Susie, ten years younger than Robert, wore a beige dress that was tied at the waist with a large black bow in front. Her brown hair was short with bangs. Her feet were bare on summer days when she played around the house. Susie loved to spend time with her friends who occasionally dropped by except today they were all busy helping around their own homes. Her lack of entertainment at home had driven her to the field to offer water to her brother.

Robert heard Susie grunt aloud as she began lowering the bucket to the ground. Just then, her fingers lost their grip of the rope handle. Water splashed everywhere including on Robert. "Sorry!" she cringed. "I thought I could do it, but my arms feel like wet noodles." Having noticed his red cheeks, soaking wet shirt, and overalls, Susie asked, "Are you thirsty?"

"Am I thirsty? What kind of question is that? Where in tarnation have you been?" Robert asked half joking. "Anyway, I asked for a drink of water, not a bath."

"Hey, that's not fair. That bucket was heavy. I didn't mean to get you wet. You didn't even say thank you."

"Thank you!" Robert smiled and lifted the long-handled silver drinking cup. It felt cool and refreshing to his lips, and he took several dips from the wooden bucket. He directed his gaze upward into the bright sunlight and said playfully to Susie, "Look! Do you see that buzzard circling over the field? You better run back to the house before he comes to get you." Susie looked up, then turned her gaze back at Robert who grinned with a smirk.

"Stop being so mean to me. And don't think for a

minute that I can't tell the difference between a hawk and a buzzard." Robert delighted in joking with his sister. For a fourteen-year-old, she knew how to stand her ground.

Seeing Susie's carefree, jovial reaction, made Robert long for his own carefree youth. He remembered how simple life was when he was still attending school. Susie had been fortunate not to have to work in the cotton factory like so many of her young friends.

"Mama will have lunch ready by the time we get back," Susie said. "Are you ready to come back?"

"Not right now," Robert objected. "Let me finish these last few rows. I might just skip lunch and meet you for an early supper. How does that sound?"

"If you say so."

She wrinkled her brow, "I don't think that Mama will like it though. You don't eat lunch with us anymore. Mama said so herself. I think she is worried about you. Should I be worried too?"

"The only worry you should have is trying to figure out if you are going to eat lunch or if you are going to become lunch for those birds up there. Now git goin'."

Susie poured out the remaining water, picked up the empty bucket, shrugged, and began walking back in the direction of the house which was visible in the distance over a small rolling hill. From a short distance, she stopped, looked back at Robert, and raised her arm to wave as she hollered, "See you at supper." Robert waved back, then made a clicking sound signaling the mule to move forward.

There was less than an hour of daylight remaining as Robert put the mule in the animal barn near the house and stowed away the plow. While still in the barn, he removed his mud-caked boots, and the dirty overalls before putting on a clean pair of pants and a fresh clean pair of work shoes. Reaching for a small towel kept near the watering trough, he grabbed a bar of soap and a bucket. He wet the towel, rubbed it with soap, and began scrubbing his arms and face Susie knew Robert's routine so well by now that she had prefilled the animal watering trough with clean water that came from a small pond on the property. After bathing, Robert exited the barn and headed towards the front porch.

The wooden clapboard house stood atop large rocks stacked on one another which served as the house's foundation raising the floor two feet off the ground. It allowed just enough space for dogs, cats, and chickens to find their way under as they sought relief from the late July sun. Standing tall above the level of the roof were two fireplaces. The first fireplace was built out of rock in what served as the main living quarters. More recently, another addition to the house provided space for a kitchen and a dining room. The chimney in the newest part of the home was made from red brick. Most family time was spent in the dining room or the kitchen. The roof was made of hand-cut wooden shingle shakes. There was a small, covered porch on the front of the house which was also supported by rock and mounded earth. The doors were solid wood, and the windows had small glass panes.

William and Martha Chambers looked through the open kitchen window as their son made his way from the barn to the house.

"It's going to be another difficult month at the tobacco auction. We are already several inches short of last year's rainfall and yesterday's shower was the first we have seen now for almost three weeks," William sighed. "Now I know why they call us clay-eaters in town. We will not be able to feed the family and keep the farm unless prices go up before we get to market."

Martha placed her hand on Williams' shoulder as she leaned in only inches from his face. Her eyes were warm, and her smile brimmed with confidence. "God will provide."

William appreciated her unwavering faith in him and in God, but right now all he could see through the window was a farm that might be lost to the bank if they couldn't continue to meet their financial obligation. "I want to believe that honey, I really do. But I wonder if our bank manager knows that. He might be praying for us to default on our mortgage so he can resell this farm to some of these new cotton growers moving to town. I heard him say that there's real money in cotton and that tobacco growers won't last much longer."

Martha didn't so much as flinch, "I refuse to believe that. We must have faith. Please don't give in to your fears. Just look at all we have to be thankful for. We have our son and daughter as well as this wonderful home you built for us."

William wrapped his arms around his wife, "What would I do without you? Even on my worst days, you are always there to make me feel better. I love you so much." He leaned over and kissed her on the cheek before they both turned away from the window and moved toward the kitchen.

Martha was well aware of farming's difficulties and uncertainties. There were so many variables that were out of their control. Most problems were caused by the weather. One year their young tobacco leaves sprouted and looked as healthy as they could remember, but they soon withered and died because of an unexpected drought. She also experienced the strain of rising at four in the morning each day to pick produce, work around the house, then prepare the meals before joining the others in the fields. Most nights she did not find relief until after nine o'clock. In addition to her daily responsibilities, Martha carried the weight of her son's misfortune. Recently she had learned from a friend that Robert was no longer dating Anna Smith, his long-time girlfriend. Robert usually shared most things with her, so why had he kept this to himself? Was he embarrassed or deeply hurt? It troubled her to know that he would not confide in her. His behavior told her that something was obviously wrong.

William had just taken a seat in his favorite chair when Robert came through the door. Robert took a deep breath and sat by his father. "How did the field look today?" William asked.

"It would not have been any trouble except the dirt was heavy and wet," Robert responded. "Got a bit wet myself when Susie came splashing by."

"That's not true," Susie laughed exiting the kitchen where she had been helping her mother with supper. "You were mean to me."

"Mean?" Robert asked looking over his shoulder. "Was it mean of me to try and protect you from the buzzards?"

Susie looked back and forth between Robert to her father, "Don't start that again. I told you those weren't buzzards."

"What's this all about?" William asked.

Robert explained the interaction between him and Susie earlier that day in the field.

"I see," William replied looking back at Susie who was now standing right behind them.

"Susie has always had a good eye. Do you remember the time I took you squirrel hunting?" William asked Susie.

"You talking about the time I saw a squirrel way over in a treetop, and you said it was just the wind blowing?"

"That's what I mean. That girl has the eyes of a hawk. She can see things that I never even knew were there."

Robert smiled and surrendered, "I give up. I can see you are both against me." Susie skipped back to the kitchen.

"You remember we talked about going into Petersburg tomorrow for supplies," William said. "I also want to go by the broker's office and see the current auction prices."

"I remember." Robert enjoyed the trips into town, but lately, it had put him on edge. He did not want any embarrassing moments with Anna's family in town. There was always that possibility when they visited the crop broker's office at the tobacco warehouse since many of her relatives also farmed tobacco. That would make for an awkward conversation in his father's presence, especially since his father would not understand why there would be conflict between the two families.

Anna had been more vocal with her family about her relationship with Robert than Robert had been with his. It's not like Robert did not want his family to know what was going on in his life, but he was often silent on such matters and figured he was doing them a favor by not sharing intimate and personal information that might embarrass them or him. For as long as he could remember, Robert had always been one to keep his thoughts to himself. He was never intentionally rude to anyone, but he was not going to spend a lot of time in conversation when he could make his point and move on. He was aware that he had never been honest with his parents about what really happened between him and Anna. He also knew that his mother was worried and when she worried, she would often ask probing questions that made Robert even more anxious than before. While he would never admit it, her questions made him realize just how angry he was with Anna. His relationship with Anna had ended suddenly following a terrible argument, and it was easier for him to try and forget about what happened than to talk about it.

Robert's mother called from the kitchen, "Supper is ready."

"Let's eat," William said tapping Robert on the knee just before they both stood up.

Robert swallowed hard and walked to the table.

CHAPTER 2

Milledgeville, GA

Elizabeth Bright pushed on the partly opened front door of the parsonage where she lived with her parents. She had just returned from work as a part-time English tutor. Now twenty-three years old, this was her last summer semester of college. Elizabeth had brown eyes, high cheekbones, and a beautiful complexion. She towered over most other girls and many of the boys as well. With an offer from an elementary school in Petersburg, Georgia, about ninety miles away, she planned to become a teacher in the fall. Elizabeth called out to her mother, then moved quickly down the hall after hearing no response and called louder, "Mother!" It was then that she thought she heard a faint whisper or moan. The sound seemed to come from the back of the house. She continued down the hall of the bungalow-style one-story home looking into each open doorway and calling, "Mother!"

Her parents' bedroom was located at the end of a long hallway just across from the kitchen. Through the open doorway of their bedroom, she saw her mother lying on the floor in a small pool of blood. Gasping, she rushed to her mother's side.

Mary Bright, Elizabeth's mother, was once an intelligent, articulate, and independent person. That was before she suffered a stroke four years earlier. Doctors blamed the stroke on her epilepsy. The onset of early dementia also complicated matters. Martin and Elizabeth had been Mary's caretakers all this time with little help from friends or hired sitters. Neither of them was sure if that was because they were so far from other family members, or if they were too embarrassed by Mary's behavior to involve others in her care. In the initial stages, Mary was able to function on her own for several years. They could leave her for hours at a time without worry. But in the last few months, epileptic seizures had resulted in falls and loss of consciousness. They had tried to ensure that they never left Mary unattended. This morning was an exception.

Just then, Martin ran through the open doorway and called loudly, "Mary!" Martin had been the pastor of First Presbyterian Church in Milledgeville since Elizabeth, their only child, was born. It was his first church out of seminary. Seminary life had been difficult for both him and Mary, but as a newly married couple, they had made the best of it. Times were hard but their love and devotion to one another was constant. Now this generous, thoughtful, and optimistic pastor was being challenged in ways that no one could see coming just a few years earlier.

"Back here, Father."

Martin stopped cold at the open bedroom door. Elizabeth was kneeling beside her mother. He couldn't help but notice the trail of blood that ran from Mary's head, and it was difficult to determine her injuries since she was still unconscious.

"Hurry, get some towels. Wet one of them," Martin shouted. Elizabeth ran to the end of the hall, quickly returning with several towels in her hands.

"Do you know what happened?" Martin looked back and forth from Elizabeth to Mary trying to calm himself.

"No, I just walked in myself!" Guilt flooded Elizabeth's mind about accepting the job as a tutor knowing that her mother needed constant help.

As Mary began to regain consciousness, they helped her from the floor to the edge of the bed and applied a cold compress to stop the blood flow from a small cut above her left eyebrow.

Martin softened his voice and asked, "Mary, what happened?"

"I don't know. I just wanted some fresh air, so I walked into the backyard. When I came back in, I went to the kitchen and . . .," Mary's voice trailed off seemingly in search of words that could not be found. "Then I walked from the kitchen to the bedroom. That's all I remember."

"Mother, why is the shovel in the house?"

"Shovel?" Mary asked sounding surprised.

Martin said, "It looks like you tripped on the shovel coming into the room. Your head must have hit the edge of the footboard. Why did you bring a shovel into the house?" The stress in the room was palpable. Martin seemed to be doing his best to maintain control of his own emotions.

Mary began to sob. Martin knelt on the floor in front of her shaking body and wrapped his arms around her. "It will be okay, sweetheart. You sit here while Elizabeth and I go to the kitchen and start something for dinner." Before leaving, Elizabeth helped her mother put on a sleeping gown and bandaged her cut. Martin picked up the shovel and placed it outside.

"Lie back on the bed and rest for now," Elizabeth said while closing the door quietly and joining her father at the kitchen table.

Martin said, "I was afraid that something like this

would happen. Her condition is getting worse. She became disoriented, and I found her in the neighbor's yard last week. I am sorry I never told you. I knew it would only make you worry."

"That's okay, Father. You are right, I am worried as I am sure you are."

Martin continued, "One of the elders recently asked if something was wrong at home because Mary had not been in church with me for the past few months. It sounded more like an insinuation than a concern."

"I am sure the church understands and would be willing to help you and Mother. You have served the members of this community with all your heart and soul for the past twenty years."

"In today's world, your job is only as secure as your last sermon," Martin said with a frown. "A member recently inquired about Mary's behavior and suggested that I might consider sending her away for a while. He insinuated that if I were not so preoccupied with Mary, then I might have more time to visit shut-ins and visitors."

"Please, not that again," Elizabeth responded. "I am tired, as I know you are, of a few naysayers in church who are never satisfied. They have no idea what you do every day, the endless hours of sermon preparation, visiting parishioners, and dealing with the constant conflict required to mediate a group of people who overall mean well though are somewhat misguided by others at times."

Martin had been a good shepherd of his flock and was affirmed by the members of the church on most occasions. He had also been a willing servant when members were ill or when family members died. In his heart, he knew that there were only a few people who complained about his work. He tried to keep that in perspective when issues arose.

"I know that you are right," Martin said. "Misguided is a good way to describe them. Some of them are just emotionally wounded people who mean well not knowing that they are projecting their pain on others. I guess that I just happen to be an easy target. Yet, every one of them is a child of God and deserves pastoral care. However, I have to admit that it is difficult dealing with negative members."

Elizabeth was feeling frustrated, but the task at hand needed her attention. "Father, we can talk about this later. Mother has already started supper. She has some fresh corn from our garden in a pot and has sliced some tomatoes. Let's get the left-over sliced chicken from Sunday's dinner and heat it up with what we already have. Does that sound good to you?"

"That sounds wonderful." Martin lifted his gaze and

reached out to pat Elizabeth's hand. His bright blue eyes were wet but clear. "Elizabeth, in all honesty, it will be difficult when you leave in August."

"Maybe I could stay here for a few more months to help take care of Mother. I am sure another job will come along sometime." Elizabeth wanted to be there for her parents just as their parents had been for them, but she also wanted to accomplish her goal of becoming a teacher. None of the schools in Milledgeville had any vacancies for new teachers, which is why she had chosen to accept a position in Petersburg that she heard about through a school professor.

"Don't you dare. You have worked hard and studied too long to let an opportunity like this get away from you. We will be fine. There are several widows in the church who would be more than happy to come and sit with Mother when I'm not at home. And I'm a rather good cook, so we won't starve."

"Father, you are always so positive. Sometimes I don't know how you do it." Elizabeth admired her father for having the grace and composure to navigate even the most difficult times, not only in their lives but also in the lives of others.

"I don't do it alone, Sweetheart."

Elizabeth continued, "You know what the doctor said about her falls. It might not be safe for her to stay in our home much longer."

"I know. We shall see. Time will tell."

"When will you visit the facility in town as the doctor recommended? I mean if she does eventually need to move out of the house."

Just on the outskirts of Milledgeville, there was a hospital that housed the elderly and afflicted. Some of the locals referred to it as an asylum. Martin was not in favor of that description, but he did have several concerns about placing Martha there. He had visited families of church members there over the years and had seen the drawn faces gawking at him through the windows as he approached. Some of the windows on the back side of the building were barred with steel rods. During his visits to the hospital, it was common for him to hear people scream out either in physical pain or mental anguish. He had heard stories that on occasion the local authorities sent prison inmates to be housed at the hospital for counseling or rehabilitation. It was not what he nor Elizabeth wanted for Mary, but because of her condition, there did not appear to be many alternatives.

"I have an appointment to meet with the head of staff at the hospital next week," Martin said.

"I don't want this any more than you or Mother, but they might be able to help us."

"I will go," Martin sighed.

"Good, Father!"

"I know that we will have to do something soon, but it breaks my heart to think of her being left there alone."

"It breaks my heart as well," Elizabeth replied.

They sat in silence for a few moments before Elizabeth stated, "I'm going to get supper ready."

"Here, let me help."

Just then, a loud thud followed by a crashing sound came from the bedroom. Elizabeth and her father jumped up from the kitchen table and rushed to the bedroom where they found Mary once again on the floor.

CHAPTER 3

Petersburg, GA

Early the next morning, Robert and his father hitched the horse to the wagon for their journey to Petersburg. The early morning air smelled fresh and clean. The humidity was low, and the temperature was more pleasant than usual.

"I see you decided to dress up for the ride to town," William laughed pointing at Robert's dirty boots and overalls.

Waving a hand in dismissal Robert smirked, "Well, who's got chewing tobacco stains all down the front of his shirt? And how long ago was it I heard you say that you gave up chewing? That looks and smells pretty fresh from where I'm sitting."

"It's your mothers' fault."

"How do you figure that?"

"Everything was fine until the preacher told me that she baked him a pecan pie. When he took the first bite, he bit down on a shell and cracked a tooth. Why, I burst out laughing and spit all over myself."

"Now if that don't beat all," Robert shook his head and laughed.

The conversation was a welcomed relief from the friction at the dinner table the previous night when Robert's mother had asked several probing questions about Anna. For the remainder of the ride, they mostly talked about the future of tobacco in a region where cotton was slowly becoming the crop of choice.

The road from Parksville, South Carolina, to Petersburg, Georgia, would take about thirty minutes traveling by wagon. The Savannah River separated the two towns. There was a ferry near Petersburg that would take them across the river.

At the top of a small hill, they stopped to take in the beauty of the winding river. They could see the ferry, and just up a small rise on the other side was the city of Petersburg. Petersburg had been one of the largest and most populated towns in the state over eighty years ago. Now the town was struggling to survive with a population that had dwindled from thousands to less than two hundred. The only remaining businesses were a small dry goods store, a tavern, a sheriff's office, a schoolhouse building, one hotel, two boarding houses, several tobacco and cotton warehouses, and the only cotton gin in the region.

"That's quite a view," William said.

"Sure is," Robert agreed. "Look, the ferry is already on our side of the river. Let's hurry down before they pull away, or we will have to wait twenty minutes for it to return."

William continued, "There's no hurry. I can see a few wagons already pulled close waiting to load up. We have a few minutes."

"You should know, as many times as you have crossed before," Robert replied.

THE FERRY OPERATED AT the confluence of the Savannah and Broad Rivers. It was large enough to hold up to four horse-drawn wagons at one time. A large rope suspended over the river was attached to trees on both banks. There were two additional ropes, one on the front and one on the back that tethered the ferry to the suspended rope. The ferryman took a long pole to push into the muddy bottom of the river propelling the flat bottom boat slowly forward. He repeatedly walked from one end to the other until the barge reached the other shore. The distance across the river was between one and two hundred yards when the water level was normal. After arriving on the other side, growers would take the Petersburg Road all the way to Augusta where the tobacco would be sold at auction.

The ferryman usually lived close enough to the river for customers to summon them by shouting or ringing a posted farm bell. Most travelers arrived on foot or by carriage paying a fare of ten cents per wagon to cross the river. On Sundays, the ferry would be loaded with ladies wearing their best dresses and hats while the men were dressed in dark pants, vests, and top hats. On other days, businessmen and fishermen shared the transport. The ferries up and down the Savannah River did not run at night due to the danger of navigating uncertain currents and unseen floating debris. Rides were usually uneventful, but everyone was aware of how dangerous the river was during storms and floods when it could quickly swell and fill with all kinds of floating trees or tree limbs which had broken free from the shore.

Less than a mile from the shore a large stately two-story house was visible a short distance from the road. The house was painted white with black shutters. It had a wrap-around porch supported by multiple columns with a wide set of steps descending from the middle. A swing suspended by chains could be seen on the right side of the front porch. A two-foot-high cement foundation with an entry point in front extended around all four sides of the home creating a low barrier. It was placed about twenty yards from the foundation of the home. Several trees were planted along the outside of the cement barrier.

"I have always wanted to meet the man who owns the ferry. He and his family live in that big house," William said.

"Sure is a might pretty place," Robert replied. "I hear they have a large family, but everyone must stay busy because I can't remember seeing anyone outside."

William spoke, "Times were good here some years ago when that home was built. The owner was a successful tobacco farmer like us. Besides this ferry, he also owned a dry goods store in McCormick."

Robert looked up at the front door of the home again expecting someone to walk out any minute and greet them.

"Let's move on," William said. "We should be about ready to load."

At the end of the road, they pulled the wagon up to the shore in a small flat staging area where the ferry customers loaded and unloaded. The exiting customers had already pulled forward onto the shore far enough to clear the path for the others who were now beginning to pull forward onto the ferry platform. Several people walked on and stood to the side while William and Robert guided their horse and wagon onboard. Once everyone was safely aboard, the oarsman leaned on the pole pushing them away from shore. A man sat on the far end of the ferry with a fishing line in the water. Beside him was a bucket of water holding a mess of crappie that would be eaten for dinner.

William walked over to the fisherman, "Looks like you are doing well?"

"Been a great day for fishing so far." Pointing towards the opposite shore the fisherman continued, "I wait until the ferry gets to about the middle of the river before I drop my line. There's an old rock bed and some brush around it where the crappie love to hide."

"Someday when I have time, I would like for you to show me how to catch crappie," William stated.

"Happy to. I try to get down here at least once a week. I can catch enough fish in one day to feed my family two or three meals. But I have to warn you, they are sneaky little devils. You have to know the exact spot and depth to drop your line; otherwise, you won't even get a bite."

"Tell me about it. That sounds a lot like one of my normal days of fishing," William laughed.

"Well, you meet me here this time next week if you can, and I'll show you how it works," the fisherman offered.

"You got a deal," William replied.

The water was so calm that the only ripples visible were those made by fish chasing dragonflies that were daring enough to fly near the surface. Although there weren't many flash floods, stories continued to circulate in town of the time when unexpected and violent rains ripped the ferry from its moorings and sent it speeding downstream casting horses, men, and wagons overboard. At least once a month, town members who gathered at the local dry goods store in town still talked about the drownings of family members and livestock that awful day. Many agreed that they would never attempt to cross the river anytime immediately after the passing of storms or hard rains. The river was both admired and feared.

After landing on Georgia soil, they continued on to Petersburg. The wagon lurched and swayed up the hill from the ruts and potholes. The building tops in Petersburg could be seen from the crest of the hill.

"Well, what did you learn from the fisherman?" Robert asked.

"He said that he would show me how to catch crappie if I meet him here next week," William answered.

"That would be nice. Crappie are one of the best-tasting fish you can eat."

William looked back up at the approaching buildings

and asked, "How about we stop by the auction barn before we pick up supplies? I'm anxious to see the tobacco prices."

"Okay by me," replied Robert noting a tone of concern in his father's voice. Robert did not have complete knowledge of the financial status of his parents. The family rarely talked openly about private issues. However, he was fully aware of how anxious they seemed to be about their current state of affairs.

From the distance, they could see the front of the Petersburg tobacco auction barn and warehouse. "They don't seem to be too busy, so maybe we can get in and out quickly," Robert added.

The barn was the largest building still standing in town. There was a long porch that was covered with a tin roof on the front of the two-story building where a few men sat in chairs. Even from a distance, Robert could see that one of the men looked like Matthew Smith, Anna's father. Robert shifted his weight in the seat of the wagon.

"You okay?" William asked.

"I'm fine. This seat is just getting hard."

Robert looked at his father, "How about you?"

"What about me?" William asked.

"Are you okay? It sounds like you are worried about the price of tobacco. Both you and Mother seemed out of sorts at dinner last night."

"I was kind of hoping that you did not pick up on that."

"Well, I did. Is everything okay with the farm? I know this has been a bad year, more like a stretch of several bad years."

"I can't deny that," William grimaced. "It seems to get harder each year to make enough to cover our expenses including the mortgage on the farm."

Robert looked ahead while adjusting his hat trying to think of what to say to his father. "I could get a job you know."

"We have talked about that before, remember? We can't afford to hire someone to replace you on the farm. There is too much work to do. You know yourself that it takes all of us, including Susie, to be able to get everything done."

Robert looked back at his father, "What if we just sold the farm and moved away from this area? We could go to Augusta or Columbia. I hear that there are lots of jobs available in the bigger cities."

"That may be true," William said rubbing his chin. "But we are farmers, always have been. I just don't think I would be happy working in a factory the rest of my life."

Robert thought about his father's words as they drew near to the front of the tobacco warehouse. It was true that farming was a tradition in his family. Did that mean they were all destined to farm the rest of their lives, even during hard times? How would he provide for his own family, assuming that he was able to have a family of his own? Based on his recent experience, he wasn't sure if he ever wanted a family if it meant being in a relationship like any of his previous ones.

William and Robert stopped in front of the warehouse, got down, tied the reins of the horse to a hitching post, and walked inside. Robert kept his head down as they entered the barn so that the brim of his hat partially hid his face from the men sitting in the rocking chairs. He hoped they would not recognize him from a distance. Inside the barn was a large open space with racks stacked adjacent to one another in long rows each filled with tobacco leaves. One side of the floor contained hundreds of bundled tobacco leaves, bound together with burlap, awaiting shipment. The open door of a train car was visible at the rear of the warehouse. Men were using two-wheel carts to move bundles toward the open door.

"Robert!"

Hearing his name called loudly, Robert and William turned to see two men approaching.

Oh no! Robert thought to himself seeing Matthew Smith, a tall barrel-chested man, approached with a scowling face. His first thought was to hide behind the tallest stack of tobacco leaves, but he knew that would only delay the inevitable.

"Good morning, Matthew," William greeted him.

"Good morning you say. How good can it be, William? Anna told us two weeks ago that your son Robert here was going to be the father of our next grandchild, at least that was until she lost the baby day before yesterday."

"What!" William gasped looking at Robert in disbelief.

"You mean he hasn't told you yet? Why does that not surprise me?" Matthew pushed back his sleeves.

"Robert, what do you have to say for yourself?" William asked.

Robert suddenly stiffened shaking his head in embarrassment almost unable to form his thoughts. He certainly knew about the pregnancy, but he was just now learning about the death of the unborn baby.

Robert once thought that he and Anna were in love, but that all ended when he heard from Frank Parks, a close friend and owner of the local general store in Parksville that Anna had been seen around town with Thomas Wright. Thomas was the son of Theodore Wright, the bank manager in Petersburg. Robert confronted Anna with the story, but she denied, at first, that she had been anywhere near Thomas. Later, she admitted that she had "bumped into him" while in town one day. It was easy to understand why men were attracted to Anna. She was taller than most girls her age, with a soft complexion, and brown hair that matched the color of her eyes. Her family once owned the largest tobacco farm in the region employing hundreds of hired hands. But just like all tobacco growers in the area, times were changing, and farms were shrinking. Her parents were very protective of their only child. Anna resisted and became a wild, rebellious teenager who seemed to always live on the edge of trouble. She made friends easily, especially with boys. As a result, her parents only became more protective. They decided to move across the river to Petersburg seven months ago from their original family farm in Parksville. It was their attempt to get a clean start both for themselves and their daughter Anna.

Robert began to feel sick to his stomach, blinking rapidly before tightly closing his eyes. He opened his eyes just as a large fist struck him in the nose. The punch sent Robert stumbling backwards causing him to trip on a stack of tobacco leaves. He quickly jumped to his feet. His arms and fists tightened ready to strike back. He began to taste the blood that was trickling from his nose and running into the corner of his mouth. Robert's father quickly stepped between the two men and grabbed Robert around the chest pinning his arms down.

"That's enough," William snapped.

"You better pray that Anna survives the complications from losing that baby," Matthew barked with a red face and flared nostrils.

Two months earlier, Anna had been diagnosed with pneumonia which resulted in her temperature spiking for several days. The doctor concluded that the loss of the baby was due to the seriousness of her illness. Her body continued to struggle to fight off the fever from the illness combined with the stress of the miscarriage.

"If she doesn't, then you better believe that I will come looking for you!"

"Hang on now, Matthew," William objected. "Robert and I will have a talk about this. I'll be in touch."

"That is if I don't get in touch with you first," Matthew growled.

"Please calm down, Matthew. I'm sure Robert can explain everything," William said putting his hand around Robert's broad shoulders pulling him away from the argument.

"You haven't seen the last of me," Matthew's jaw tightened. He breathed deeply.

William and Robert moved away from Matthew putting distance between them and his murderous stare. Robert walked outside wiping his bloody nose. His face was throbbing. They made a brief stop for supplies at the local dry goods store before getting in the wagon to take the road back down to the ferry.

They rode in silence about halfway back to the river. Robert struggled to find the right words to say to his father.

William spoke first, "We can talk about this whenever you are ready."

"I am sorry," Robert replied. "It's just not true. You know that Anna and I spent time together, but there is no way that I could be the father of her child."

"I believe you Son, but it will be hard to convince her family."

"I don't think her father will ever believe me," Robert guarded his words carefully. Most people in town were not aware of Anna's reputation. However, he did not want to do or say anything that sounded judgmental of her even though he was angry with her for starting such a nasty rumor. They continued to the ferry in silence both men lost in their own thoughts and feelings.

After crossing back over the river, they encountered a wagon coming from the opposite direction. The driver looked to be a few years older than Robert. He was tall and fit. His deeply set eyes looked as dark as his jet-black hair with the brim of his hat tilted slightly down. He was wearing a nice three-piece suit and polished boots. Riding along in the back of his wagon were a dozen workers, both male, and female. The white lint in their hair and the croaker sack pouches hanging around their necks made it obvious that they had just come from working in the cotton fields.

As the wagons drew close to one another, the driver smiled politely and nodded.

"How was the ferry ride?" the driver asked.

William answered, "It was fine. We watched a man reel in a large catfish."

"Oh, forgive me for not introducing myself first. My name is Simon Hale. I own the local cotton gin and warehouse in Petersburg."

"Nice to meet you! I am William and this is my son Robert."

Looking at Robert's swollen eye, Simon said, "What happened to you? Did you run into a fence post?"

"I'm fine," Robert answered sharply. He wanted to tell the man to mind his own business.

"Are you farmers?" Simon asked.

William said, "We have a small tobacco farm just on the other side of Parksville."

"Tobacco!" Simon moaned. "Don't you know that the most productive farms around here are planting cotton? Tobacco is on the way out. Cotton is king. Tobacco farming is too risky anyway. Did you hear about the tobacco curing barn in Parksville that recently burned to the ground? They found the body of the owner's son in the ashes three days later. Still don't know what happened."

"Yeah, we heard," Robert snapped looking directly at Simon. He was well aware of the fire and the loss of one of his friends.

Simon's eyes widened lifting his eyebrows, "I didn't mean to upset you. I was just trying to warn you."

"Josh was my friend, and we don't need to be warned." Robert's anger was rising. It may have been because of his throbbing eye and nose, or the stranger's attitude that set him on edge.

"I'm sure he don't mean no harm," William said looking from Simon back to Robert.

"Well, you boys take care; I've got to get these workers back to town," Simon stated.

As the wagons began to part, Robert noticed that Simon had a bullwhip beside him on the seat and a Smith and Wesson revolver holstered to his side. Simon's parting smile made Robert uncomfortable.

William said, "That was interesting."

"That's one way to put it," Robert replied. "It's hard to say, but something about that man bothers me. I can't exactly place it. Maybe it was the way he addressed you so informally."

"I don't think he's from around here," William said.

Robert thought about his friend who died in the fire and the investigation that continued. They still didn't know if it was an accident. If it wasn't, then what could have happened? Experienced farmers were accustomed to tending curing fires in their tobacco barns without incident. The community was in turmoil over the recent tragedy. They were further distressed about the unforgiving drought which had lasted for years.

Normalcy was no longer an expression that accurately described their lives. Threats to life as they once knew it seemed to be coming from all directions. Outsiders were bringing change to the communities and there seemed to be a never-ending flow of people moving across the river from South Carolina. With some of the new people came new and dangerous businesses that were beginning to gain traction. The black-market bootleg industry was growing dramatically each month as more farmers turned to dis-tilling spirits as opposed to growing crops or livestock. Robert knew that his father was opposed to the infiltration of moonshine and whiskey in their community. He had made a public plea at a town meeting encouraging citizens to stand up and fight to keep the county dry.

Nearing the outskirts of Petersburg, Robert and his father noticed smoke coming from the direction of their farm.

CHAPTER 4

Milledgeville, GA

The horse-drawn carriage stopped in front of a set of cement steps that led from the road up a long sidewalk to the building's entrance. Near the road, a sign read, "Mid-State Hospital." Martin clutched a small suitcase, exited the carriage, then turned to offer a hand in assistance to Mary and Elizabeth as each stepped out.

The sixty-year-old brick facility sprawled across twenty acres surrounded by pecan trees and fields. It was a large structure located just on the edge of Milledgeville. Standing three stories tall, the main building spanned wide on both sides of the main entrance. Small-paned windows crossed the front, with at least twenty windows per floor in both directions. Windows on the extreme ends of the facility were covered with either metal bars or meshed metal. The main covered entrance was supported by six tall columns spanning from the first to the third floor.

Martin knew the facility well, but this was the first time that Mary and Elizabeth had visited it. Elizabeth and her father had already discussed his previous visit with the head of staff. Both were still grieved over the thought of leaving Mary behind in this place, but with her epileptic fits and mental confusion, they both knew that they could no longer properly care for her at home. Nor could they find anyone willing or able to stay with Mary.

At the front entryway, a tarnished bronze plaque mounted to the wall read, "Mid-State Lunatic Asylum." The letters had faded so badly that they were barely visible. Elizabeth took one glance at the plaque and then quickly looked away willing herself to unsee what was now seared into her mind. Mary shuffled past without even noticing.

"You okay?" Martin asked.

"I think so," Elizabeth answered.

The hospital once housed some of the most mentally ill patients imaginable from all over the state of Georgia as well as surrounding states. They were also known to accept prisoners from the Milledgeville jail upon request from the local sheriff. When the asylum first opened in 1837, the staff developed a reputation for using unproven and dangerous methods of treating patients with shock therapy and binding restraints.

Most of the patients lived out their lives at the asylum, and many died young because of either their illness or the treatments. Some referred to the treatments as experiments. Looking from the windows on the third floor, one could see hundreds of grave markers in a large open field. Each headstone was alike, standing tall and narrow. Four numbers were etched into each stone designating the patient numbers of former asylum residents. There were no names or dates, only identification numbers.

Fortunately for the community and patients, the hospital had come under new leadership and was now operated by a conscientious Hospital Board. The new staff members took pride in the care of their patients as well as the care of the facility.

Martin pulled the front door handle and stepped aside allowing Elizabeth and Mary to enter the reception area. A sterile, clean smell greeted them. The reception area was brightly colored with lofty ceilings and neatly hung paintings. The rocking chairs were plentiful. Near the front, an older woman dressed in a white nurses' uniform sat behind a large desk.

"Good morning! How can I help you?"

"Yes, good morning to you as well. We are here to see Mrs. Hudson. My name is Martin Bright."

"Did you have an appointment?" the uniformed lady asked.

"Yes, we did," Martin answered.

The receptionist looked back and forth between all three of them, smiled, and stood. "I'll be right back."

Martin looked nervously at Elizabeth and then at Mary. Mary walked over to investigate a colorful painting elegantly framed and hung from high above using long strands of wire. It was similar to one hanging in the parsonage.

Elizabeth whispered to her father, "Are you sure this is right for Mother?"

"I can't say if it is right or wrong," Martin responded. "But it is necessary! We have both seen how her fits are now occurring daily. The only people who we thought could help us are afraid of her behavior."

"Maybe we can go back and try again to find someone," Elizabeth sighed in a hushed tone. "I'm still willing and able to take care of Mother."

"Shush, here they come," Martin said placing a finger to his lips. "We can talk about this on the ride home."

They could hear two sets of footsteps approaching

just before Jane Hudson, head of staff, turned a corner and came into view closely followed by the receptionist. Jane approached with outstretched arms. Her smile was warm and comforting.

"Nice to see you again Pastor," Jane said. She took both of Martin's hands in hers.

"Hello Mrs. Hudson," Martin replied.

"Please, call me Jane!"

"Of course. Jane, this is my wife Mary and our daughter Elizabeth."

Jane looked first at Elizabeth and shook her hand warmly, "Nice to meet you, Elizabeth." Then she raised both arms again reaching out to Mary whose hands were tightly clasped in front of her. Mary slowly raised her hands.

"How are you today, Mary?" Jane asked with compassionate sincerity.

Mary's red and puffy eyes were fixed in a distant stare. She looked up for the first time since going over to gaze at the painting but did not make direct eye-to-eye contact with Jane. She opened her mouth to speak, but no words came forth.

Elizabeth's lips were pressed together in a slight grimace. Tears had formed in the corner of her eyes. It was as if she no longer recognized her mother who was standing right in front of her. Mary's illness had manifested itself late in life and had aggressively caused a downward spiral at a dizzying pace. The fits were now occurring multiple times a day. Their family physician had not been encouraging. He told Martin that Mary only had a small chance of living more than a few months.

Jane invited them to follow her to an office where the admittance process began. The silence was deafening. They proceeded down the long corridor. Disbelief flooded Elizabeth's mind throughout much of the process. Martin asked several questions to which Jane confidently responded that Mary would receive the highest level of care and comfort possible. Room and board for most patients cost a little over one hundred dollars a year, except for those who required more intensive care. After they signed all the forms and completed the final arrangements, Jane led the threesome back into the reception area. Once again, she reassured the family that Mary would receive the best care available. Then she took Mary by one hand while carrying her suitcase in the other and slowly began to lead her down the corridor. Elizabeth covered her mouth with a light gasp, and tears trickled down her cheeks. She watched her mother walk away without even so much as a proper goodbye. They both stood there as the minutes painfully and agonizingly ticked away on the grandfather clock near the front door. Finally, without speaking, they turned and slowly walked out.

Elizabeth took one final look over her shoulder while the carriage wheels rattled beneath them on the road back to the parsonage. Martin's eyes were fixed on the road ahead and his shoulders slumped in grief. He weakly attempted to comfort Elizabeth who sobbed uncontrollably for most of the ride home. The summer humidity was evident, even at mid-morning as the carriage arrived back at the parsonage. Martin exited first, then assisted Elizabeth. He had dealt with grief his entire career, seeming to always know what to say to others, but at that moment words escaped him. Elizabeth had also experienced grief when her grandparents died, but that paled in comparison to how she felt at this moment.

They walked onto the front porch of their home. Martin pointed towards the two rocking chairs inviting Elizabeth to sit down with him. He looked at Elizabeth making eye contact with her for the first time since leaving the hospital, "As hard as this is for us, I still believe that we did the right thing."

"I know you're right, but this is so hard," Elizabeth whispered. Once again her eyes turned downward, and her chin quivered. "Father, please let me stay with you until Mother improves or...," she pleaded. Her words trailed off, unable to accept the possibility that her mother may never return home.

Martin reached over and took Elizabeth's hand. They sat lost in their thoughts for a moment. "Look at me," Martin implored with the soft comforting voice of an experienced pastor. "Your mother and I raised you to be the responsible young lady that you have become. As difficult as this may sound to you now, one day you will thank me for encouraging you to stay the course. I believe that God has called you to Petersburg, and if God has called you, then God will also equip you. We all live out our lives one day at a time with the grace that God has given us, knowing that there are no guarantees for tomorrow. Today's worries should be enough, and we would be better off by not allowing ourselves to worry about tomorrow. I have learned that I am happier if I can release my worries about the future to God, trusting that God knows what's best for my future even when I can't see it myself."

Elizabeth thought about her father's words. She knew that he was right, but in her heart, she still felt torn. What purpose could God have by calling her to leave her family at this critical time in their lives? How could she ever discern God's will for her life?

Martin continued, "I'm going in to prepare something for lunch. If you're like me, I'm sure you don't feel hungry right now, but it would be best for us to eat a little something. You are welcome to sit here and enjoy the sunshine for as long as you like."

Elizabeth smiled, "Thank you, Father. I think I will sit here for just a few more minutes."

"Take as long as you want. I'll see you inside."

Elizabeth had always enjoyed sitting on the front porch of the parsonage. It didn't seem that long ago when her mother or father would help her into the rocking chair, her legs dangling unable to reach the floor. She looked over at the swing where she had spent hours on Sunday afternoons with friends after church. She smiled remembering the first boy who kissed her sitting right there in that same swing. Closing her eyes, Elizabeth allowed the memories to play out in her mind with the same color and vibrance of the past. Tucked in the corner of each memory was the presence of her mother. These thoughts caused even her happiest memories to make her feel sad. She opened her eyes and exhaled deeply. Wiping the tears away, she looked up feeling a new sense of determination to not let the circumstances interfere with what she knew she must do. She stood, straightened her dress, and turned towards the front door to join her father inside.

CHAPTER 5

It was common to see smoke coming from a fire-cured tobacco barn. There had been incidents where barns had been lost to fire, but it was exceedingly rare. Many of the local growers cured their tobacco in small barns built mostly from logs cut and shaped on the property. In low fire-cured barns, a small fire was built and allowed to smolder for as much as ten weeks to promote the curing process. Hardwoods were used as firewood to add the desired flavor and color to the final product. Fire curing normally produced tobacco low in sugar and high in nicotine which was highly desirable for pipe tobacco, chewing tobacco, and snuff.

The billows of smoke that filled the northeastern sky

seemed to have a never-ending trail which was an obvious sign that this fire was large and out of control.

William and Robert's wagon moved as fast as a freight train as it drove through the center of Parksville kicking up dust and rocks. Joseph Davidson, the sheriff of Parksville and Robert's classmate looked out the window of his office in time to see the horse-drawn wagon thundering past. Joseph kicked back his chair from the desk so hard that it turned over backward. He grabbed his rifle from the rack hanging on the wall and ran out the front door where his horse was tied and saddled. Joseph rode hard and fast but still did not gain on the wagon until he came in sight of the Chamber's tobacco barn. Flame leaped from openings in the roof and billowing smoke rose high into the sky.

Rumbling to a stop they saw Martha and Susie frantically running back and forth from a nearby watering trough with overflowing buckets. They were wet from head to toe and appeared exhausted.

"Hurry!" Martha screamed. The three men ran towards the burning barn.

The structure's size was insignificant compared to the animal barn. It was just large enough to hold all the tobacco leaves from the Chamber's field at harvest time. If the fire had been detected soon enough, there would have been a good chance of saving the building and the crop. But this fire was red-hot and had been burning far too long.

Once the watering trough had been emptied, they began to run back and forth from a small pond near the house. It quickly became evident that they could not save the barn because the distance was too great and the buckets too small. Standing alongside his friend Joseph, Robert bent over with his hands on his knees. William stood coughing and snatching deep breaths. He rubbed the back of his neck with a handkerchief. All of their eyes were red, and tears stained their cheeks. They stood and watched in anguish as their main source of income went up in smoke.

Even though Robert was still young, he understood the devastation and financial hardship this would cause his family. He also knew that they needed the income from this crop to live through another winter on the farm.

Martha's arms were tightly wrapped around the front of her body as if attempting to hold herself together.

"We couldn't have been gone twenty minutes," she managed to whisper with a shaky voice. "I'm so sorry."

William walked over and wrapped his arms around his wife. She rested her head on his chest. He held her tight and whispered, "It's not your fault."

"This never would have happened if Susie and I hadn't left home this morning."

Martha and Susie departed early that morning to walk over to an adjoining farm. Their neighbors had struggled most of the year with illness and hardship so Martha thought that they might appreciate some fresh eggs from their hen house. Upon arrival, they were invited to come in and eat breakfast. After breakfast, they had only walked a short distance when they saw the smoke. Both Martha and Susie ran all the way home to find the fire raging out of control. Hearing Martha's story, Robert and his father understood how the fire could have burned so long without being seen. But no one could understand how the fire started in the first place.

William tried to console Martha who struggled to maintain her composure, "We don't know that. You were doing what you thought was right at the time."

By now, both Susie and Martha were crying. The family was dependent on the income from the crop. They were experienced in curing tobacco by fire. Each of them had nurtured the small fires both day and night during the curing season. Everyone knew that a disaster like this could occur, but it was unlikely since so many precautions were taken to prevent the curing fire from escaping its confinement.

Robert immediately became suspicious and began to look around for any evidence that might support the idea of the fire being started intentionally. Considering all possibilities, several questions flooded his mind. He walked around the perimeter of the smoldering building looking for tracks made by man or beast. He had not found any evidence that was distinctive until he reached the ground around the side of the barn that would not have been visible from the house. An imprint made by the sole of a large boot was still intact in wet red clay. Robert was able to follow the prints just a few yards into a pine forest where they faded away disguised by the thick layer of pine straw that blanketed the area. With the trail cold, he could only assume that whoever made those tracks had either walked or ridden alone on a horse that must have been tied somewhere close.

When Robert returned, his family had gone into the house to clean themselves up. His friend, Joseph, was standing on the front porch waiting for him.

Wiping his friendly-looking face with a clean towel, Joseph asked, "See anything out there?"

"Maybe, but I can't be sure."

"We need to talk," Joseph said with concern. "Do you remember the loss of the Martin farm and the death of our friend Josh?"

"Sure," Robert replied.

"I was told by someone I trust that Thomas Wright had visited Josh only a few hours before the fire was seen coming from their barn," Joseph explained.

"Well, they were friends once just like us. Why is that so important?"

Joseph leaned in, "My source said that they had been overheard arguing a few days earlier. I was told that it almost came to blows."

"What was it all about?" Robert asked.

"That part is not real clear, but it seemed to have something to do with your girlfriend Anna."

"Anna!" Robert growled. "She's not my girlfriend."

"I know that. Don't get upset with me. I think Josh may have been defending you thinking that you were still seeing Anna. It makes sense to me that the two of them would have argued if Thomas told Josh that he had been out recently with Anna."

Robert knew that Anna had been seeing other men. That was the reason for their breakup. However, he was not aware that Anna had been going out with Thomas while he was still dating her. He had begun to suspect that she could not be trusted, but the fact that she had been cheating on him was more than disturbing.

"Wait!" Robert said. "Are you thinking that Thomas had something to do with the fire and Josh's death?"

"I'm not ready to go that far yet. This is all still a part of my investigation. You must keep this between us. Don't share this information with anyone or my case may fall apart."

"I understand!" Robert's thoughts were racing faster than their wagon had minutes before. In some ways, he could see something like this coming, but he never imagined that his former girlfriend and an accomplice could have been involved in arson and murder. He was well aware of Anna's reputation, and it wouldn't surprise him if she was seeing someone else. He knew she had been acting indifferent towards him. But now he was wondering how long this might have been going on.

"I need to get back to the office," Joseph said. "Remember, don't discuss this with anyone, okay?"

"I won't."

Joseph rode away, leaving Robert sitting alone on the front steps of the house. The pain of Anna's possible deception kept him awake at night, and it now caused a twisting ache in the pit of his stomach. He tried to take in everything that had happened today including this new revelation about Anna, and he decided that he had been silent enough. As painful as it was for him, he knew he would soon have to talk to his family about his relationship and falling out with Anna.

Robert heard the front door gently open and close behind him.

"Your mother is so distraught; I am worried about her," William said to Robert joining him on the steps. The pungent smell of smoldering ash and tobacco filled the air.

"What are we going to do?" Robert asked.

His father's gaze was transfixed on his hands which were clasped in front of him, "We will just have to learn to take one day at a time. It was just the other night your mother told me that I needed to have faith."

"Do you?" Robert asked.

"What is faith?" William asked. "Is it something I can turn on when things go well and turn off when they don't? Or maybe I have that all backward. I don't know. I heard the preacher once say that faith was believing in things that we can't see or touch. What I see in front of me causes me to have more fear than faith. If faith can produce miracles, then I'd say we are in much need of it."

"I can tell you that I have faith in you. You have never let this family down, and I know you won't now. We will figure this out together."

William looked up into his son's eyes and placed his

hand on Robert's knee, "You are all very precious to me, and I believe that we will be able to overcome this loss. If that's faith, then yes, I feel like I have enough to endure this storm."

"Let's go in and check on Mother and Susie. They need to hear this as well, especially now."

CHAPTER 6

Milledgeville, GA

Less than a month had passed since Mary had been admitted to the hospital at Milledgeville. Her health continued to rapidly deteriorate. She was now in a coma. Elizabeth spent most of her time at her mother's side. When she or her father was not at the hospital, a volunteer from town stayed with Mary.

Late one evening Martin and Elizabeth sat at their dinner table listening to light raindrops making percussion-like sounds on the tin roof. Elizabeth felt guilty about leaving her mother at the hospital that afternoon, but she understood the importance of self-care. Elizabeth needed food and rest. The constant worry and caregiving demands had exhausted her. She had always been close to her mother who had been the playmate of her youth and her primary support throughout life. She dearly loved her father, but being a pastor kept him away from home more than anyone wanted. For the past month whenever Martin was not at the hospital, he spent time writing sermons or visiting church members.

Elizabeth shuttered at the thought of facing tomorrow without the love and tender care of her mother. She missed those times when life was filled with happiness and hope for the future. One of her treasured memories was the delicious strawberry birthday cake her mother always made for her. She looked forward to it each year. For Elizabeth's most recent birthday, Martin asked a parishioner to make a strawberry cake, but it wasn't the same. Missing out on those special times was what Elizabeth now dreaded the most. Everything was different now. During her last visits to the hospital, Elizabeth often wondered if her mother even knew who she was. The blank stares and confused looks were the only forms of communication that Mary had been able to muster.

Elizabeth was telling her father about the events of the day when there came a light knock on the front door. Mrs. Hudson had dispatched a staff member who lived in town to stop by the Bright's home to tell Martin and Elizabeth that they needed to return to the hospital as soon as possible. They feared that Mary might not live through the night. It had been several days since Mary had been able to swallow, and she had not eaten anything for over a week.

The carriage ride between home and the hospital that evening seemed to take an eternity. It had been raining most of the day. Thunderclaps rang out like the gong of their church bell. Windswept rain pelted their faces with stinging intensity, saturating their clothes.

The hospital finally came into view. Elizabeth gazed into the haze and rain and caught sight of something that looked odd. It appeared as if someone was running from the hospital towards a nearby field. The figure had only appeared for a moment when the sky was briefly illuminated by yet another flash of lightning. She blinked rapidly and tried to convince herself that it was only her imagination created by a falling limb or blowing object. She did not say anything to her father about the disturbing image. The carriage slowed stopping near the front entrance. They quickly secured the wagon and ran to the entrance.

Once inside the dimly lit reception area, Martin and Elizabeth stood as small puddles of water began to form around their feet. It was eerily quiet. Most of the patients and staff appeared to be at dinner. Light danced and flickered from the candles and lanterns that were either placed on tabletops or mounted to the wall. Martin and Elizabeth slowly proceeded down a long hallway when the silence suddenly burst into loud disruptive screams. The voices were misplaced and awkward. Normally, the hospital had been unusually quiet. They soon learned that the screams were not coming from a patient but from a hospital staff member.

Suddenly, a woman in a nurse's uniform sprinted into the hallway almost falling forward as she rounded a corner. There was a look of sheer panic on her face. She looked one way and then the other. In her distress, she had not noticed Martin and Elizabeth standing in the hallway.

"What's wrong?" Martin called out trying not to alarm her any further.

The sound of Martin's voice shook her from near hysteria. The nurse stopped suddenly and turned in their direction. Her eyes continued to dart from side to side. Breathing heavily, she struggled to speak, "Two of our patients from the local jail have escaped."

"Where are they now?" Martin asked.

"One of them ran out a back door, but the other one has not been seen. Be careful. They are both dangerous. I have never liked the idea of allowing criminals to be treated here." She sprinted down another hallway leaving them alone again.

For the next few minutes, they stood in silence not knowing what to do.

"Stay with me until we reach your mother's room," Martin whispered quietly.

They proceeded until they reached the doorway to Mary's room only to find that she was not there. The bed was empty, and the sheets lay crumpled on the floor. Startled, Elizabeth wondered if they were already too late. Why was her mother not in her room? Could she have already passed away? Why would they have moved her? How were the two of them going to find her with so many rooms and hallways? Without the help of a receptionist or staff member, they were on their own to figure out Mary's whereabouts. They chose the first long corridor on the right which was absent of people. Most of the on-duty staff were away from their normal posts either in hiding or assisting in the search for the escapees.

"Are you going to be okay?" Martin asked Elizabeth.

"I think so. At least for now."

"Stay behind me." Martin pulled Elizabeth close.

The two of them walked slowly, carefully stopping at the door of each room long enough to take a quick look. One, two, three rooms passed with no sign of Mary with what looked like twenty-five more to go just in that corridor alone.

It did not take Elizabeth long to figure out that they might never find her mother with so many rooms in each direction that covered three floors of the hospital.

"Father," she pleaded. "We need help. Let's go back and wait for the receptionist or another nurse to return. Nobody knows we are here except the nurse we just passed near the entrance."

"You're right," Martin replied.

As they turned around towards the reception area, Elizabeth saw a shadow beginning to emerge on the floor of the main entrance hallway. Shadows could be deceiving based on the location of the light, but Elizabeth thought that by all indications this shadow fit the body of a large person moving slowly towards the exit. They stiffened and quietly backed against the wall as a hand, then an arm appeared in the opening. Elizabeth sucked in a quick breath. The hand was holding a large kitchen knife. By now the full figure of a large muscular man stood less than forty feet away looking directly at them. His hair was brown and stringy touching the back of his shirt collar. Even from a distance, Elizabeth could see a jagged scar on his left cheek. He turned with a noticeable limp in their direction just before the sound of a voice boomed down the hallway behind the man.

"Ridley! Stop or I'll shoot!" a night guard shouted. The

shout distracted the criminal. He took two steps back into the main hallway eying Elizabeth and her father. Suddenly, he turned and ran towards the front doors of the building. The convicted criminal, James Ridley, had finally found his opportunity to escape and had disappeared into the night. James was not a particularly smart man, but he was smart enough to know that if he could convince the sheriff that he was mentally unstable or suffering from an injury, then he would have a chance of being transported to the hospital, dramatically improving his chance of escape. The plan had worked perfectly, and now he was on the loose.

The guard ran past the hallway where Elizabeth and her father stood frozen against the wall and pursued the criminal out the front door. Suddenly, the breathless night guard ran back inside. Seeing Martin and Elizabeth standing in the main hallway he asked, "What are you doing here at this hour of the night? That man could have killed you."

"We are here to see my wife, Mary Bright, who is a patient. Mrs. Hudson sent for us."

The guard responded, "I think I saw your horse and carriage racing away. The convict must have taken it. Stay right here and let me find someone to help. Whom did you say you came to see?"

"Mary Bright!" Martin spoke emphatically.

Elizabeth peered out the front door through the falling rain. Just then a streak of lightning briefly illuminated the front lawn of the building. The guard was right. Their only transportation back to town was gone.

In a few minutes, the same nurse who had previously stumbled into them returned and approached Martin.

"Are you pastor Bright from Milledgeville?"

"Yes!"

"I am so sorry. Nothing like that has ever happened here before. Are you okay?"

"We are or at least I think so. Can you help us find my wife? She is not in her room."

"Yes, I know where they moved Mary. Please follow me!"

They looked at each other, then back at the entry door as if expecting the man with the knife to walk back in, but he had fled with their horse and carriage.

The nurse led them to the end of the first corridor of the West wing where a staircase was located. Martin and Elizabeth followed, occasionally looking over their shoulders until they reached the third-floor landing. They followed the nurse down a dimly lit corridor. She paused at an open door stepping aside to allow Martin and Elizabeth to enter. A single candle near the window was lit. An empty chair sat next to Mary's bed.

The nurse spoke softly, "We moved Mary here about an hour ago. She was having difficulty breathing, and we thought she might be more comfortable on an upper floor where air seems to circulate better."

"I was told that an aide was to be stationed here at all times!" Martin said firmly with a frown.

"Yes, we have kept an aide here with Mary around the clock. Perhaps she stepped away during the raucous. I'm sure she will be back soon."

Elizabeth watched in horror as her mother struggled to breathe. It had only been a few weeks ago that Mary had walked unassisted into the hospital. Elizabeth wondered if this might be her last opportunity to tell her mother how much she meant to her.

"Mother," Elizabeth called, but Mary was unresponsive. She leaned in close to Mary's ear and whispered, "I love you!"

At that moment, the nurse's aide returned and apologized for leaving, assuring them that she had only been away for a few minutes.

"That's okay," Martin spoke with assurance. "How is she?"

"I am sorry to tell you that she has declined quickly over the past few hours. I debated whether I should tell

Mrs. Hudson to call you back to the hospital. You never know about these things. But I thought you both needed to know that she was getting worse by the moment. Please don't be angry with me."

"Of course not, I understand," Martin replied.

"To be honest Reverend Bright, I didn't think you would get here in time."

"Thank you for contacting us. We are grateful that we are here now."

The aide looked at them while pointing to a spot in the corner of the room. "I can help you make two pallets on the floor with blankets and pillows if you want me to."

Martin answered, "That would be fine. It is late and we are very tired."

"I will be right back." She returned in a few minutes with several thick blankets, sheets, and pillows.

"I'm sorry, but we don't have any available beds on this floor."

"This will be fine until morning," Martin responded.

They reclined on the pallets hoping to rest if they could only shut off their thoughts. Elizabeth's eyelids were heavy, but sleep seemed to evade her for a long time. The events of the day were stealing any opportunity to sleep. Every time she closed her eyes, she saw the vision of the man with the knife turning towards her. Her mother's breathing faded in and out. It seemed like minutes passed between breaths.

———

"ELIZABETH," HER FATHER WHISPERED several times.

"Beth!" he said a little louder.

When Elizabeth opened her eyes, she could see flickering light from the candle. The wick was short, and the flame had begun to fade. Soon there would be no light in the room.

"How long have I been asleep?" she asked.

"Maybe an hour or two," Martin responded.

She sat up and blinked clearing her vision. There was just enough light for her to see the glistening eyes and quivering chin of her father who was now sitting in the chair by the bed. He was holding Mary's hand. He seemed to be drowning in a sea of grief.

"She's gone, Beth!"

CHAPTER 7

Petersburg, GA

Robert and his father moved the last piece of furniture into the house the family would now call home. Following the loss of the tobacco barn over a month ago, they were unable to make the mortgage payments. The Parksville bank president was a long-time family friend, and it was evident that this was painful for him as well, but the bank's board of directors left him no choice. The loan was already three months past due at the time of the fire. When the bank foreclosed on the property, the Chambers family had to find a new home and new jobs.

Fortunately, William was able to secure work as a ferryman on the Savannah River. The salary was not enough for the family to live on, but the fact that they could live in the home of the previous ferryman without rent was a blessing. The house was located close to the river, which benefited both the ferryman and his customers. It was much older and smaller than their previous home but was adequate for now. It was located on the opposite side of the river from Parksville which made the larger town of Petersburg more accessible. Robert and his father were hopeful that they would be able to financially recover in a few years and buy another farm.

After settling in, Susie and her mother cleaned the house while Robert borrowed the family horse and wagon for a brief ride back to Parksville. His father assisted by providing a ferry ride across the river.

"I'm going to see if Mr. Parks can help me find work," Robert told his father while easing the wagon off the edge of the ferry platform touching the ground in South Carolina.

William looked at Robert, "Okay Son, tell Frank I said hello." William's eyebrows furrowed and his gaze turned downward, "Again, I'm terribly sorry about all this. I will make it up to you. Thanks for all your help and for understanding."

Robert could hear the despair in his father's voice. It was late in life for his father to have to start over again. Robert also grieved for himself. He was committed to helping his family, but at the same time, he knew that he wanted a family of his own. He felt unsettled about changing between a life of commitment to his parents and sister, or a life devoted to his own family. He struggled to sort it all out on his ride to Parksville.

Above the tree line ahead, he could see charcoal-colored smoke billowing from the train's engine long before he felt the rumble of the oncoming train. The friendly engineer waved at the people on the roadway which paralleled the train tracks. The train made a stop in Parksville before proceeding north toward the next stop in Vienna.

Robert gazed into the windows of the passenger compartments as the train sped past. He wondered about the lives of the travelers. The men wore brimmed hats, and the ladies wore dress hats of all different shapes and colors. From a distance, they seemed to be enjoying themselves. Some even waved to him through the windows. Robert wondered if their lives were anything similar to his.

Under his breath, he mouthed to himself, "What am I doing wrong?" What would it be like, he thought, to have that kind of money and freedom? Robert longed for the day when he too could afford a trip on the train and get a break from his obligations back home. He did his best to shake off the negative thoughts that were swirling in his head. He entered the own and pulled up at the general store.

Frank Parks, a well-known businessman in the community, owned a dry goods store in Parksville. When Robert was a young boy, he loved to ride to town with his father to get supplies so he could look at the candies and toys in the dry goods store. On each visit, Mr. Parks would slip a piece of hard candy into Robert's hand, with a smile and a wink. Frank always smiled and joked with his customers. Most everyone knew him as a kind, jovial man who frequently extended credit for groceries to local families in distress. Some people thought that Parksville was named after Frank, but the similarity was just a coincidence.

The dry-goods store in most communities not only provided food and clothing but also served as the local post office, town hall, and the center of social life. Parks Dry Goods was a two-story building with the second story serving as Frank's residence. Frank never married. He lived alone.

In the back right corner of the first floor was a large pot-bellied stove used to heat the store in the winter. Near the stove was a used pickle barrel where locals sat around and played checkers at night. Several wanted posters were tacked to the wall near a window that served as the post office.

Frank was dressed in his usual attire. A white

apron covered his clothing and spectacles were perched on his nose.

Seeing Robert walk through the front door, Frank called from behind the counter, "Robert my boy, how are you?"

Robert waved and answered with a friendly greeting and a warm smile. "Hello, Mr. Parks. It's been a while."

"It certainly has been. What brings you in today?" Frank asked.

"Actually, I came to ask you a question."

"I heard about the fire, and I have been worried about you and your family. How are your mother and father holding up?"

"We're okay for now. Father found a new job, and we moved into the ferryman's house this morning."

"Yes, I think it was just yesterday I heard that William was going to be our new ferryman. Well congratulations, Son. He will do an outstanding job."

"Thank you, Mr. Parks, I am sure he will," Robert replied. "Now, about that question?"

"Sure thing, Son. How can I help?" Frank stopped sweeping the floor and looked at Robert.

"My father doesn't know exactly why I came to see you, so it would be nice if we could keep this between us. I told him that I wanted to ask if you knew where I could find some work. But I really need to ask you if my family owes you money. As you know, we lost the farm when we couldn't pay the mortgage."

"To be honest Robert, most of the local folk owe me something. Some more than others."

"I want to help pay our debt just as soon as I find a job," Robert said.

"Tell you what, I may be able to help with that. Do you know Fred Taylor?"

"I know the name. I've heard about his cotton farm, but I don't remember meeting him."

"Fred is a close friend of mine. He's a good and honest man. He's looking for someone to help oversee his hired hands who work in his cotton fields."

Robert silently rejected the idea of working in cotton. He was still bitter about how the cotton industry had pushed many of his neighbors, who farmed tobacco, out of business. Large cotton farms were cropping up all over the area, and he had seen firsthand how cruel the work bosses were to the workers in the fields. It was not unusual to hear the sharp crack of a whip, or a gunshot fired overhead while passing cotton farms located close to the roadways. He remembered the recent encounter with a cotton boss named Simon the day he and his father were returning home from Petersburg.

Robert smiled while trying to hide his true feelings, "I might just stop by on my way home and talk to Mr. Taylor."

Like it or not, Robert needed a job. With the decline of local businesses and no farm of his own to work, he knew he did not have many options. Cotton factories were springing up in the region offering jobs to many. But in order for him to work in any of the factories, he would have to move. None were close to Petersburg.

Frank continued, "Since your father will be around the ferry most days, there is something else you need to know."

Pointing at one of the wanted posters on the wall Frank said, "Have you ever seen that man around here?"

Robert looked intently at the rugged face of a man with a large scar on his cheek. The caption above the drawing read, "James Ridley - Milledgeville Escapee."

"I don't think so. He's an ugly cuss!" Robert replied.

"Tell your father to watch out for this one. He was born in Vienna which means he may be trying to get back to this area. He is nothing but trouble. I know that some folks from Vienna will be using the ferry as they cross into Petersburg for supplies."

"I'll be sure and tell him," Robert said. "By the way, you didn't answer my question. Does my family owe you money?"

"As I said, my boy. Most everyone around here owes me something. As far as your family, it does not amount to much. I am confident that your father will not allow his debt to go unpaid, so don't let that worry you."

After thanking Mr. Parks for the job referral and directions to Fred Taylor's home. Finally, Robert said goodbye, then turned to walk out. Just before he reached the door, he heard Frank call his name. Looking back, he saw Frank walking towards him with two stuffed croaker sacks, one in each hand.

"Take this with you," Frank encouraged while handing Robert a bag of flour and a bag containing cured ham.

"But I...," Frank held up both hands interrupting Robert in mid-sentence.

"It will be on your account until your first payday."

"Mr. Parks, this is not necessary," Robert said.

"All the more reason why I want you to have it son. Your father and I go back a long way. I count him as a good friend. I'm not one bit worried that William Chambers will let a debt go unpaid."

Even though it had been many years since visiting Frank's store, it was obvious that Mr. Parks was the same loving and generous man he had always been.

"I don't know what to say except thank you. I will pay you back."

"I'm not worried. You can give me a portion of your first paycheck from Fred Taylor. Take care," Frank replied.

Robert tipped his hat to Fred, walked out, placed the supplies behind the seat in the wagon, and drove away. During the short ride to Mr. Taylor's home, his thoughts spun like a whirlwind. He knew that opportunity was knocking, but he had a bad impression of the cruel cotton bosses. He turned down the road leading to Mr. Taylor's farm and wondered if this job would be right for him.

CHAPTER 8

After talking with Fred Taylor, Robert headed home. He stopped briefly at a ridge top to take in the fresh air and look down on the beautiful flowing water that snaked slowly through the valley. Bright yellow blooms of goldenrod wildflowers waved with the rhythm of the wind in the unplowed fields. The cooler breeze signaled the coming of fall. It would still be a few weeks before the leaves started to change into vibrant autumn colors then ultimately lose their life-giving attachment to the limbs and fall gracefully to the ground.

Even from this distance, Robert thought he recognized his father on the nearest shoreline preparing to meet customers traveling from the South Carolina side of the river. Robert and his father had been avid tobacco farmers. He was not looking forward to telling him about his new job as a cotton foreman. Based on his reference from Frank Parks, Mr. Taylor offered him a job earning ten dollars a week for the first ninety days. Robert felt that Mr. Taylor was an honorable businessman who treated others with dignity and respect. He also learned that he made no apologies about his expectations for profitable results. Robert was impressed with the way Mr. Taylor conducted business, and he hoped to be able to learn more about the cotton business from him. He was scheduled to start on Monday of the following week. Most of Mr. Taylor's cotton fields were in Parksville or Vienna on the South Carolina side with only a few in Petersburg.

The ferry pulled up to the shoreline just as Robert arrived. His father was standing in the middle of the ferry platform, speaking with departing customers and collecting fares. Robert counted two cotton wagons, one supply wagon, and one stagecoach onboard as well as ten to twenty people. Some of them were stepping onto their wagons or mounting horses, as others began walking to shore. Robert watched his father greet each customer and ask for their names. After everyone unloaded, the reloading process began. Once everyone was onboard, William again walked the length of the ferry to greet customers as an assistant used a pole to push the ferry forward.

The stagecoach was on the opposite end of the ferry from Robert's wagon. It was difficult to see inside, but the passenger appeared to be a woman wearing an elegant hat. After landing on the other shore, the driver of the stagecoach pulled forward slowly onto the flat loading area and stopped.

Robert also unloaded and pulled his wagon over to the side away from any oncoming traffic as he stepped down and stood close enough to hear the end of his father's conversation with the stagecoach driver.

"What happened to Buster?" the driver asked looking down at William. Buster, the ferry's former owner, had known most everyone in town after serving as a ferryman for over ten years.

"Buster moved back to Augusta to help take care of his family members still living there," William answered putting his hand above his eyebrows to shield the sun.

"You know, he did tell me that he had family in Augusta. I liked Buster," the driver replied.

"Well, given time, I hope that you will like me, too. Where you headed?" William asked.

"I'm taking this young lady to the boarding house in Petersburg. She said she's the new schoolteacher in town," he said politely looking over his shoulder.

"Pleased to meet you, ma'am," William tipped his hat while looking through the open window of the stagecoach.

"Nice to meet you as well, Mr...," she hesitated.

"Mr. Chambers, mam. William Chambers. That's my son, Robert," he said pointing towards Robert who was now standing closer.

"Hello Mr. Chambers, my name is Elizabeth Bright. I will be teaching at the school in Petersburg." After a tearful goodbye with her father, Elizabeth boarded a train in Milledgeville and arrived in Vienna some four hours later. She and her father had discussed at length whether Elizabeth should stay in Milledgeville. He assured her that he would be fine living alone and that he felt comfortable knowing his church members would keep an eye on him.

Elizabeth would be co-teaching with another young professional who had been employed for a short time. Very much like the town, the school population had also been shrinking. On most school days there were only about twenty-five children attending the five-room schoolhouse built when Petersburg was thriving. The children were now split into two classrooms. Elizabeth would be instructing the older students.

"Do you have any children who might be attending school this year?" Elizabeth inquired.

"Yes mam," William answered. "My daughter Susie will be enrolling this year. We just moved from Parksville, and she's excited about meeting some new friends."

"Did Susie have an enjoyable experience in the Parksville school?"

"We had a school building once, but it was destroyed last year by a cyclone. That's another reason that my wife Martha and I are excited about living here. We did the best we could from home, what with all the farm chores. The only schooling Susie had last year was done by us at night," William added.

"And what about Robert?" Elizabeth asked, tilting her head in Robert's direction. "He looks to be about my age. What does he do?"

Robert had been a good student with a bright future, but that was before a severe drought and famine hit the Broad River area. Farmers were the most negatively impacted, so Robert dropped out during his last year of school to take odd jobs. After dropping out, Robert's parents bought used schoolbooks from friends whose children had already finished school. They did their best to work with him at home. It was not much trouble since he enjoyed reading and learning. His favorite subject was history.

"Robert's smart. He can do anything he sets his mind

to," William answered. "Right now he is helping me and our family as we build a new life here in Petersburg."

"Sounds like we're both starting a new life here. I don't know much about Petersburg."

"I'm still learning my way around the ferry, and Robert has been looking for a new job for himself."

"What happened to your old life, if you don't mind me asking?"

"That's a long story. I can tell your driver is in a hurry to get you into town. Why don't you come back and see us now that you know where we live? We would be happy to share a meal with you and tell you all about it."

"That sounds wonderful," Elizabeth responded with a smile.

After paying the fare, the stagecoach driver began to slowly move forward. Robert looked through the window and saw the young woman who he thought was the most beautiful person he had ever seen. Elizabeth looked up after closing a small purse. The angle of the sun allowed the light to gently dip into the stagecoach compartment. Elizabeth raised her hand over her eyes to get a better look at the face of the young man standing on the roadside. Robert tipped his hat in recognition of the passenger. Elizabeth looked intently at Robert and gently tilted her head.

"Who was that woman riding in the stagecoach?" Robert asked his father.

"That's Elizabeth. She's our new schoolteacher," William replied. "I invited her to come back and have a meal with us sometime."

"What did she say?" Robert asked, trying not to sound too interested.

"She said yes, of course."

Even though the new schoolteacher was beautiful, Robert tried to ignore her as the coach pulled away. He no longer trusted women. His experience with Anna had made sure of that. He had no plans to get involved in another relationship, or at least not for a long time. Life would be simpler for him if he let someone else court the beautiful schoolteacher. He figured that his buddy Christopher would be chasing after her in no time.

—

AFTER PASSING THROUGH TOWN, Elizabeth's coach began to slow in front of a white two-story house. A wrought iron fence stretched across the front and sides of the lot with a swinging gate in the middle. The boarding house where Elizabeth planned to spend the next year of her life had stately porches on the front of both the ground and second floors. A friendly looking woman with silver hair sat on the ground floor porch in one of several white rocking chairs.

The driver assisted Elizabeth who stepped down to retrieve her suitcase. After paying her fare she walked towards the house.

"You must be Miss Bright," the lady said while standing.

"Yes, and you must be Mrs. Norman?"

"Most people call me Kate."

Both ladies smiled. Kate Norman was gentle and friendly, which made Elizabeth feel welcome. Following the death of Kate's husband, she decided to rent rooms in the house that was much too large for her needs. Their children were grown and had moved away to other towns in search of work. She led Elizabeth inside the entry foyer and asked her to place her bag on the floor near the stairs. Once inside, Elizabeth saw a staircase ascending the wall on the right side. Near the top of the stairs was a landing that turned with a few additional steps that ended at the second-story foyer. On the lower level, doorways to rooms were visible on both sides of the foyer. There was a sitting room through the first opening on the left. The back bed-room on the ground floor served as the personal residence of Mrs. Norman. A dining room with a long table and a built-in China cabinet was on the right. Each room con-tained a coal-burning fireplace with beautiful mantels and small pastel ceramic tile hearths. Mirrors hung above each mantel. The back porch had been enclosed creating a hallway that led to a small kitchen with a wood-burning stove.

After the full tour, Elizabeth was escorted to one of four upstairs rooms. The room was not large, but it was cozy and offered enough space for her to be comfortable.

"Does this suit you?" Kate asked.

"It will be perfect."

"Dinner will be served soon. I'll ring the bell."

"Thank you, Kate."

Elizabeth unpacked her suitcase and hung up some of her things in the cedar-lined closet, putting everything else in a chest of drawers. On top of a low-profile chest was a ceramic bowl and large pitcher along with a mirror. She closed the door to her room and changed out of her dusty clothes.

The August humidity was stifling stealing any feeling of comfort in the upstairs bedroom. She raised the window and cracked the door hoping to improve the airflow, then lay down to rest for a few minutes. She was awakened with a start from a knock on the door. Standing in her doorway was twenty-four-year-old Ruth Garrett. Ruth was about to start her second year of teaching at the school in Petersburg. Her shoulder-length curly blonde hair was tucked under a bonnet which was tied under her chin with a pink ribbon. She was smartly dressed though not as attractive as Elizabeth.

"Are you Elizabeth?" Ruth asked excitedly.

"Yes, I am!"

"It's so good to finally meet you," Ruth said still standing in the doorway. "Mrs. Norman told me that you would be coming soon. Do you like your room?"

"It will be adequate."

"I asked Mrs. Norman to put you in the room on the same side of the house as mine so that way the afternoon sun would not shine in your window, but I guess she just couldn't work it out. Such a shame. You're going to roast like a Thanksgiving turkey on this side of the house," Ruth concluded with a slight smile and giggle.

"Thank you for trying," Elizabeth said.

"Well, I will let you get back to your nap. Supper will be served in fifteen minutes. See you downstairs."

"Thanks again."

Elizabeth lay down on the bed and closed her eyes. Questions flooded her mind. Why hadn't she disobeyed her father and stayed in Milledgeville? Would she be able to adjust to living away from home for the first time in her life? How difficult would it be for her to make friends with Ruth or anyone else for that matter once she started working? And what about the handsome son of the ferryman she just met? How would she be able to adapt without the companionship and love of her mother? Tears rolled softly down her cheeks. She hated the idea of her father being alone. But before she could sink deeper in thought, the dinner bell roused her. Elizabeth got up, washed her face in the ceramic basin, breathed deeply, and walked downstairs.

CHAPTER 9

By the end of summer, every able-bodied man, woman, and child, in the region, was busy harvesting the last crop of either tobacco or cotton for the season. Most students were required to work in the fields each day after school.

Elizabeth and Ruth taught in separate classrooms. Elizabeth was just learning her students' names. The older children were a delight, but she was particularly fond of Susie Chambers. Elizabeth remembered meeting William, Susie's father, at the ferry on her first day in town. She thought that Susie was fun and witty for her age and found out that Susie and Grace Bowman were good friends. Grace's parents, John, and Gretta Bowman had been friends with the Chambers family for many years. Their family had also moved from Parksville to Petersburg. Much like William, John desperately needed to find a new career following an unsuccessful attempt at farming. Elizabeth had learned that Susie and her mother were at Grace's home in Parksville the day the Chamber's tobacco barn burned down.

Elizabeth was teaching arithmetic to her class of twelve students when Gretta Bowman suddenly burst through the door and stumbled into the room. The door hit against the frame with such force that it startled everyone. Gretta was panting so heavily that she could not speak for a moment. Bent over at the hips and waving her arm in Grace's direction, she attempted to force air from her lungs to call out to her daughter Grace.

"Mama!" Grace spoke softly with a look of shock.

"Mrs. Bowman is something wrong?" Elizabeth's voice rose to a pitch.

"John has been hurt!" That was all Gretta could manage to blurt out. "Grace, we have to go!" John had been working at the cotton warehouse for less than a month. Grace stood up, collected the books on her desk, and stared questioningly at her teacher. Susie instinctively stood as well, but Elizabeth kindly asked her to sit down.

Looking back to Grace, Elizabeth said, "Go on, Grace. It will be all right." She sought to remain calm in handling her first emergency at school. Grace stood petrified unsure of what to do or say.

"It will be okay. I will check on you after school. Now go ahead with your mother."

Grace ran to her mother who was reaching out for her hand. They left the school slamming the door shut on the way out. Elizabeth gathered her thoughts and continued the lesson with the remaining children.

After school was dismissed for the day, Elizabeth asked Ruth about the location of the Bowman's home. Ruth gave her directions saying that it would take about fifteen minutes to walk to their place. Elizabeth graded a few more papers, put them in the desk, and began walking to Grace's home. Nearing the home, Elizabeth could see that there were several horses tied out front along with two horse-drawn wagons. She picked up her pace. Stepping onto the porch, she reached for the door handle. A short balding man wearing glasses and carrying a black bag was on his way out.

"Are you the doctor?" Elizabeth asked.

"Yes, I am."

"How is Mr. Bowman?"

"He is gravely injured and still unconscious. I think a broken rib has punctured his lung. It's a bit of a miracle that he is still alive."

"What happened?"

"The story is that he was unloading a cotton wagon at the warehouse in town when he got pinned against the dock by a wagon. The warehouse owner is inside."

"How awful," Elizabeth replied.

"Excuse me mam, but I have to go now. I have another appointment in town," the doctor said stepping off the porch.

"Of course doctor. Thank you."

Elizabeth pushed the door open slightly and called Gretta's name just as Gretta walked out of the family bedroom. She apologized for having to take Grace out of school so suddenly, admitting that she panicked and did not know what to do.

"I understand Mrs. Bowman. You do not have to explain."

Looking at Elizabeth with downcast, teary eyes Gretta said, "Grace is in her room, and I am sure she would love to see you. It's the closed door on the left. She's been crying for the last hour."

"Don't worry about school right now. I can catch Grace up whenever you feel it's time for her to come back."

"Thank you so much," Gretta responded.

Elizabeth turned towards the room when out of nowhere a man appeared standing right in front of her.

She was unable to keep herself from bumping into him.

"Mam!" the gentleman spoke tipping his hat.

"I'm so sorry about that. I didn't know you were standing there. Are you the warehouse owner?" Elizabeth asked.

"Simon Hale, and yes, I am. You don't have to apologize. I haven't been this close to such a beautiful young woman in a long time. I don't recall seeing you around here before."

"Oh no, I am the new schoolteacher in town. I arrived about three weeks ago."

"Your name?"

"Oh yes, sorry again. My name is Elizabeth Bright. I moved here from Milledgeville."

"Elizabeth Bright from Milledgeville. Well, my, my, it is certainly nice to meet you."

Elizabeth's face reddened. She was obviously flattered by the kind words of the stranger. She looked up at him, and when their eyes met Simon said, "Why Elizabeth, if I didn't know better, I'd think you're blushing?"

She felt the warmth in her cheeks and did not want to admit the obvious, nor did she want to let Simon in on her thoughts.

"Can you tell me what happened?" Elizabeth asked sounding a bit flustered.

"John was helping unload cotton onto the dock at

the warehouse. The driver of the wagon backed up not knowing that John was standing there. He was pinned between the wagon and the dock."

"How horrible!" Elizabeth glanced at the door where she was headed. "Excuse me, I need to speak with Grace now."

"Of course. Nice to meet you, Miss Bright. May I call you Elizabeth?"

"Yes, please do."

Simon spoke briefly to Gretta then walked outside. Elizabeth thought it was kind of Simon to visit Gretta and check on John's condition.

Elizabeth knocked lightly before turning the knob and slowly opening the door to Grace's room.

"Grace?" She whispered. Grace was lying face down on her bed with her face buried in a pillow. Hearing Elizabeth's voice she slowly raised her head. Hair partially covered her puffy eyes and Elizabeth could see the tear stains on the pillow. Elizabeth entered and knelt beside the bed. "Hi Grace," Elizabeth whispered wrapping her arm around Grace's shoulders. Grace slammed her face back into the soft pillow. Her body jerked with every sob. Elizabeth had seen her father minister to the grieved on so many occasions. She knew the best thing for her to do right now was to remain silent and just hug Grace until she was able to talk. Several minutes passed before Grace gained her composure and sat upright. Elizabeth was still kneeling.

Drying her tears Grace looked at Elizabeth through bloodshot eyes, her chin quivering, "Is my daddy going to die?"

"I am praying that he will be okay. The doctor said that he needed rest," Elizabeth answered.

"My daddy prays with me every night before I go to bed," Grace said.

"I know this is hard for you but right now I want you to take care of your father and help your mother around the house. Don't worry about school. We can work together on any assignments that you might miss. I will be praying for all of you."

"Okay," Grace spoke softly looking down at her feet.

"In the meantime, I want you to wash your face and go outside and play in the beautiful sunshine for a little while. It will make you feel better." Elizabeth kissed Grace on the forehead and walked back out into the main living area leaving the door open behind her.

"I asked her to go out and play," Elizabeth told Gretta.

"I can't thank you enough for making the effort to walk all the way out here today. It means so much to us as I know it does to Grace."

"It was my pleasure."

Elizabeth offered to come by their home to tutor Grace after school until her father improved. After saying goodbye to Gretta, Elizabeth walked outside where she found Simon standing near the last remaining horse-drawn wagon.

"Can I give you a ride back to town?" Simon asked.

"No, but thank you. It's not that far."

"Look now, I won't hear of it. Here, let me help you get up."

Elizabeth paused, looked up at Simon, and smiled before extending her hand. During the ride, Elizabeth learned that Simon relocated to Petersburg from Atlanta over a year ago to capitalize on an opportunity to expand his business. Simon once owned a small cotton operation just south of Atlanta. He told her that the cotton business was booming in the Broad River area, so he decided to move. Cotton mills had become the largest employer for most small communities in the region. It did seem odd to Elizabeth that Simon would move to a town that was clearly in decline. Soon after arriving in Petersburg, she began to hear the stories and see the results of a shrinking population. She tried to clear that thought from her mind.

By all accounts, Simon seemed to be thriving financially. He was well-dressed and owned a home in town.

Elizabeth thought that he was handsome and charming. She enjoyed their discussion on the way back to town and agreed to have dinner with him soon. Simon drove the wagon up to the front entrance of the boarding house.

"Here we are," he said.

"Thank you for the ride, Simon. I enjoyed getting to know you," Elizabeth said while turning in the seat to look at him.

"Happy to help. Let me help you down." Simon walked around to assist Elizabeth. When her foot reached the ground, it landed on the edge of a large rock hidden in the grass causing her to stumble and fall into Simon. Simon smiled broadly as he caught her in his arms.

"Well, that was real lady-like," Simon quipped.

Elizabeth straightened up, pushed back, then burst out with laughter for the first time since her mother's death. The emotions bubbled to the surface and leaked from her eyes. She was somewhere between laughing and crying, and it felt wonderful. Her face turned redder than a late summer tomato. She regained her balance and thanked Simon for catching her. Simon's arms felt strong and stable. At that moment, she realized that she was still holding Simon's hands. She didn't want to admit it, but his large hands made her feel safe somehow.

"You owe me now so don't forget about having dinner

with me. I will call again one day at the end of school," Simon added with a warm smile.

"No, I won't forget. Thank you, Simon. I look forward to our dinner together."

"So do I. I hate to leave you now but it's getting late. I need to get back and see how the rest of my workers are doing before it gets dark. It was a pleasure meeting you, Elizabeth." Tipping his hat and mounting the wagon, he steered away in the direction of the warehouse. A short distance down the road, he looked back and waved.

Elizabeth thought to herself that Simon was a nice man, not to mention handsome. She was already looking forward to joining him for dinner. She was somewhat embarrassed about her fall, hoping that Simon knew it was accidental, not intentional. But she had to admit that the laughter felt good. Smiling, Elizabeth walked to the boarding house feeling better than she had in months.

———

PASSING THROUGH TOWN, SIMON looked beyond the swinging doors of the tavern and saw one of his workers, standing at the bar. He stopped the wagon and walked inside. The tavern was filled with smoke and noise as many of the locals were enjoying drinks and card games. Small round tables lined both sides of the entryway that ended at a solid wooden bar with a brass foot rail running the full length of the bar. Simon approached the man who was enjoying a shot of whiskey while he engaged the bartender in conversation. The man saw the reflection of Simon in the large mirror mounted behind the bar. He turned and took a few steps toward Simon.

"Well!" the man said swallowing so deeply that it appeared as though his Adam's apple might fracture the bottom of his chin.

Simon looked both ways and then cut his eyes at the bartender to be sure he could not hear their conversation.

"He's unconscious!" Simon told the man whose eyes appeared to be having trouble focusing.

"Does that mean he's dead?" the man asked.

"No, you idiot! It means he's still alive. Do you still stand behind your story that he saw the cases hidden in the load of cotton?"

The half-drunken man nervously wiped his nose on his shirt sleeve and continued, "Yes, I think, or at least I believe he did. I don't know." The man was visibly shaken. His mind appeared to be running slower than the words he spoke. "All I know is that I saw him bent over, reaching into the load of cotton. That was right before I came to your office to let you know what I saw. I'm quite sure he saw the moonshine."

"Pretty sure," Simon snapped. Saliva spewed from his mouth. "You better be damned sure! If he pulls out of this and starts talking, you're a dead man," Simon's dark snake-like eyes burned a hole in the man's skull.

"It's not my fault, Simon. It was your idea in the first place. I ain't never killed a man before."

Simon glanced again at the bartender with a reassuring smile.

"Outside," Simon barked at the man. The man threw back the last of the whiskey in his glass and clumsily followed Simon through the doors.

Sheriff Davidson had been suspicious of the transportation of moonshine from South Carolina into Georgia. Even though it was not illegal to sell whiskey in Georgia, pressure from the Federal Government was slowly squeezing the profits from local moonshiners. Many distillers had been squeezed out of the business altogether. The community was pressuring the local Petersburg sheriff to take action to curtail the movement of spirits into the county. Simon stumbled on the opportunity long before moving to Petersburg, and he was exploiting its riches as one of the few remaining distributors of moonshine. There was only one other man, besides this drunk employee, who knew that Simon was illegally selling and distributing moonshine across state lines.

"Get on!" he commanded motioning to the wagon seat.

Turning away from town, Simon, and his drunk companion rode into the darkness.

CHAPTER 10

During her walk home on Friday, the mid-October temperature chilled Elizabeth to the bone. It had been an exceptionally long week. She had visited families in the community who were suffering from a flu epidemic. One of her more encouraging stops was at the home of a young man who had recovered and would be returning to school on Monday.

Mrs. Norman, the boarding house owner, had cooked fresh turnip greens with cornbread and fried chicken for her boarders that evening. Ruth joined Elizabeth at the dinner table along with a traveling insurance salesman who had arrived in Vienna by train that afternoon. The three of them shared information from the day's events, but the salesman's stories were no competition for the two schoolteachers' anecdotes and jokes from the classroom.

After patiently listening to the two ladies' incessant talk of children, just before the peach cobbler was served, the young man apparently had all he could take and announced that he was going to retire for the evening. He stood and pushed his chair under the table, leaving Ruth and Elizabeth alone at the table.

"So, you visited some families with sick children after school this week. Have you visited Susie Chambers yet?" Ruth asked before taking a sip of coffee.

"I plan to see her tomorrow, of course, that is assuming I can find an available carriage on a Saturday. It would be a long walk to the river from here."

"It is a long walk. She has such a wonderful family," Ruth continued. She did think highly of Susie's family, but the one who occupied her thoughts was the older brother Robert. Ruth met Robert not long after his family relocated to Petersburg, and she sought to win him over with a little flirtation. However, Robert had been less than kind to Ruth when her advances had become more flagrant with each encounter.

"Have you met Susie's older brother, Robert?" Ruth asked.

"Actually, I have. He and his father were on the ferry when I arrived in Petersburg for the first time. Mr. Chamber's invited me to join them for a meal."

"What did you think?" Ruth asked again.

"About what?"

"About Robert, silly. That is one handsome man." Ruth raised her eyebrows as she took a sip of coffee.

"Yes, I guess so. He was standing away from the stage-coach as I talked with his father. He didn't seem to be interested at the time."

"Well, that doesn't surprise me," Ruth continued.

"What does that mean?"

"Why don't we save that story for another time? We could be here all night," Ruth said with a smile that seemed more mischievous than sincere.

Elizabeth got the impression that Ruth was hiding something from her. Ruth was a capable teacher, yet at times she seemed quite immature. Elizabeth desperately wanted to develop a friendship with Ruth since they would be seeing one another so frequently. Even though her first impression may not have been what she had hoped for, Elizabeth knew that teaching would be unpleasant if she had to spend so much time with a co-worker whom she did not like. She decided to try and keep their conversation going thinking that her perception may change once she got to know Ruth better.

They talked shop and laughed long after Kate Norman had cleared the table. Kate interrupted their laughter for a moment and handed Elizabeth a letter that was post-marked Milledgeville GA.

"This came for you today. You two ladies enjoy the rest of the evening. I am going to bed now."

Elizabeth immediately recognized her father's hand-writing. Even though she and Ruth were having a good time, she asked to be excused anxious to read the letter from her father before going to bed.

"Good night, Ruth. Will I see you at breakfast in the morning?" Elizabeth asked pushing her chair back and moving towards the hallway that led to the stairs.

"I wouldn't miss it. Good night," Ruth answered taking a sip of coffee.

A warm glow from the coal-burning fireplace wel-comed Elizabeth as she entered her room. Kate had taken time to light the fire as well as a small kerosene lantern that sat on the desk. The fire cast a soft light in the room illuminating the small ceramic tiles that formed the hearth. A few pictures and trinkets adorned an ornate mantel that had been previously painted with multiple coats of white paint. Elizabeth sat in a chair in front of a mahogany-stained fold-down desktop and opened the letter from her father.

Beth,

I pray you are well and adjusting to your new life in Petersburg. Please write and tell me more about your teaching career. Are you comfortable at the boarding house? You must have made new friends by now. How is that going? How's the food? It surely must be hard to beat your mother's cooking.

I miss you and your mother tremendously, but I try to keep my chin up. There are many needs in the community. Do you remember Mrs. Lamar? She passed away a few days ago. I remember you telling me that she was one of your favorite teachers in school and that you wanted to become a teacher because of her influence on your life. It was not an unexpected death, but her family is still distraught as you might expect.

I thought about you last Sunday when I rang the church bell to begin our worship service. You were always so good at pulling the rope on the bell for us when you were here. Do you remember the time I had to look out the church door and tell you

that that was enough now and that you could stop?
The memory made me smile. Some days it seems like
my life has been reduced to nothing but memories. I
never knew that being alone could be so hard. As you
know, I gain energy from being with people. I receive
occasional visits from people at church, and many of
them are helpful, but it's not the same without you
and your mother here every night.

I can't say when I might be able to visit you, but
I am ever hopeful that it will be soon. Please know
that I love and miss you dearly,
Love, Father.

Elizabeth wiped away her tears, then put the letter back inside the envelope. She sat silently with her head bowed and eyes closed for what felt like an eternity. Questions flooded her mind about the decision to stay in Milledgeville or move to Petersburg following the loss of her mother. If it was at all possible, she would be willing to catch the next train back home. But she could not abandon her students. Her relationship with them was improving with each passing day. The fireplace embers grew dim. She changed into a gown and slipped under the bed covers. She lay awake for a long time staring into the darkness before sleep came.

—

THE NEXT MORNING AFTER breakfast, Robert and his father conversed about the farm before starting their day.

"How's the new job going?" William asked.

Robert had been working for Mr. Taylor on his cotton farm for a few weeks now. His opinion about the cotton industry was changing every day. He believed that Frank Parks had been right about Mr. Taylor; he was a thoughtful and compassionate man.

"I can't believe I'm saying this, but I am beginning to enjoy working in cotton."

William responded, "You're right. I can't believe it."

"It's hard work alright, but no harder than what we've been doing all these years. The thing I like most about cotton is that the product goes straight from the field to the buyer. That means the cotton growers get paid soon after the crop has been harvested. They don't have to handle the crop again like we do when we dry the leaves. Mr. Taylor told me that one of the primary reasons he was growing cotton now was because it improved his cash flow."

William listened intently and responded, "There are risks for sure, but I reckon cotton could be easier than tobacco. I shore nuff would like to be paid as soon as the crop is picked."

Robert told his father the story of the small cotton farm that had been repossessed by the bank following the sudden death of its owner. Although Robert might be somewhat of an introvert, he was blessed with enthusiasm and a desire to succeed. He had witnessed first-hand the risks of farming tobacco, but he had no plans of letting that deter him from achieving his own dreams. Even though his formal education was cut short, Robert was blessed with exceptional common sense and was not afraid of hard work. He was always the first one up and out the door each morning ready to take on his chores from daybreak to sunset.

After he and his father finished breakfast, he decided to ride to the bank and speak with the bank manager about leasing the small cotton farm. He did not want to delay knowing that the bank closed at noon on Saturdays. Robert expressed his interest in the farm and the bank manager explained the repossession process. They wrapped up their conversation before shaking hands.

Robert was encouraged as he walked out of the bank into the sunshine and got in the wagon. About a mile from the edge of town, he noticed someone walking ahead of him.

From the distance, it appeared to be a woman. He recognized Elizabeth whom he had met at the ferry.

"Where you headed?" Robert asked slowing the wagon alongside Elizabeth.

"I was going to pay a call on Susie. Aren't you Robert, her brother?" Elizabeth asked.

"That's me. I'm on my way home. Let me help you get on and you can ride with me," Robert offered.

"Stay there, I can manage," she said. She reached for the rail on the end of the wagon seat and pulled herself up. "I'm glad you came along. I enjoy walking, but your home is quite a way from town. Two days ago I walked to the Bowman's, but fortunately, another nice man offered me a ride back."

Robert said, "I need to go and see John and Gretta myself. Maybe tomorrow. My father told me about the accident."

"His injuries were extensive. I pray he recovers. By the way, how is Susie?" Elizabeth asked.

"Thanks for asking," he said. "She didn't sleep much last night but was feeling better this morning. She seems to be improving."

"Even though I have only known Susie for a short time, I have to admit that she has become one of my favorite students."

"That is kind of you to say. She is a special little girl,

and I feel blessed to have her as a sister. We joke and tease each other all the time."

"You mentioned work. What is it that you do?"

"I am working for Mr. Fred Taylor. He owns several cotton fields around here."

Elizabeth nodded, "What is it that you do for Mr. Taylor?"

"I help him keep an eye on his fields and the people who work for him. I used to farm tobacco with my father, at least that was before the fire."

"Fire?" Elizabeth asked.

"Our tobacco barn caught fire burning up all the leaves we had stored inside. We not only lost the barn, but we lost the farm as well when we could no longer make the mortgage payments."

"Oh, Robert! I am so sorry," Elizabeth responded.

"In the meantime, I took a job working for a local cotton grower."

"In the meantime?" she asked with a quizzical look.

"I don't plan to work for someone else the rest of my life. I would like to have my own farm someday," Robert said.

He looked at her and responded quickly, "Did you teach somewhere else before coming here?"

Elizabeth explained that she was a recent graduate from Georgia College in Milledgeville where she lived with her parents. At the time, the primary focus of Georgia College was to prepare young women for careers in teaching.

Robert asked, "What are your future plans?"

Elizabeth quickly questioned, "What do you mean by that? This is my future plan."

"What I meant to say is that by now you have probably figured out that Petersburg is not the town it used to be."

"I have heard some of those stories, but as long as families make this their home, then there will always be a need for someone to teach their children."

Robert was getting the impression that Elizabeth was independent and more than capable of fending for herself.

"What are your future plans, Robert Chambers?" Elizabeth turned the tables on Robert catching him by surprise. "You mentioned farming. Do you have other plans besides farming?"

"I'm working on that. There's a nice little cotton farm for sale that I would like to purchase. Actually, I spoke with the bank manager about it this morning."

"Are you sure that's a good idea in such a depressed little ol' town like Petersburg?" Elizabeth was enjoying this mental game of checkers.

Robert could not help but laugh out loud after seeing the wry smile on her face. "You got me there."

"I wasn't just referring to farming. Do you have a girlfriend?" Elizabeth asked turning towards Robert.

"You are bold. I will give you that. To answer your question, no, I do not," Robert spoke emphatically looking ahead at the road instead of at Elizabeth.

"That seemed to strike a nerve. Is there more to that story you want to talk about?" Elizabeth asked.

"Not really. Let's just say I'm enjoying being single."

"Fair enough," Elizabeth said.

"What about you? Did you leave any broken hearts back in Milledgeville?"

Elizabeth took a deep breath, "I think the only broken heart I left back home belongs to my father. Oh, I dated a boy from church a few years ago, but we grew apart once I started college, and my father and I were busy caring for my mother. I guess he eventually gave up and moved on. He left Milledgeville to move to Athens where he enrolled at The University of Georgia, and I haven't seen him since."

—

AFTER THEY REACHED ROBERT'S home, he invited Elizabeth inside.

"Miss Bright!" Susie called out as soon as she saw Elizabeth.

"Hello, Susie." Elizabeth spent the next thirty minutes talking and laughing with Susie and Martha.

"It sounds like you are feeling much better," Elizabeth said looking at Susie.

Susie's mother answered, "She is much better today. I think she will be returning to school next week." Looking at Susie she asked, "Don't you think you are ready to go back to school?"

"I can't wait to see my friends again and to spend the day with Miss Bright. She is the best teacher ever," Susie exclaimed with glee.

"A teacher is only as good as the student," Elizabeth replied.

Elizabeth already felt a close connection to the Chambers family and would not say it out loud, but she was especially fond of Robert.

"Thank you so much, Miss Bright, for coming all the way out here. It's pretty obvious that you have impressed Susie and based on the way Robert has acted, I think you have made an impression on him as well."

"You have a wonderful family. I'm looking forward to our next visit."

"Please come and have supper with us sometime." Martha continued.

"Oh yes, Robert was telling me about your fried chicken. My mother made the best fried chicken ever. I will look forward to enjoying yours as well."

Elizabeth walked over to Susie, bent down placing her hand on Susie's shoulder, "I am happy that you will be coming back to school on Monday. We can work together to catch you up on anything you might have missed."

Susie smiled, "Thank you, Miss Bright. I will be the first one in my seat. Father always said the early bird catches the worm, but I never seen that. I guess I sleep too late."

Elizabeth and Martha laughed. "See you soon," Elizabeth said turning to walk out.

Robert walked out the front door with Elizabeth and offered her a ride back to the boarding house. He invited her to join him for dinner a week from Sunday.

"I'm sorry, but I already have dinner plans that night."

"Just my luck. Who's the lucky guy?"

"His name is Simon."

"Simon Hale?"

"Yes!"

"How well do you know him?" Robert asked.

"We met recently at the Bowman's home. He offered me a ride home."

"Simon was there?"

"Why yes! After all, he is Mr. Bowman's employer."

"That's true, but…"

"But what?" Elizabeth interrupted.

"Nothing. It's not important." Robert chose to keep his thoughts to himself. He did not want to upset Elizabeth with his negative impression of Simon.

"Robert, I'm not a mind reader. Is there something you're not telling me?"

"Not really," Robert said softly as they rode in silence.

The carriage pulled up in front of the boarding house. "Thanks for the ride," Elizabeth said before stepping down from the wagon.

"My pleasure," Robert answered. "I would like to call on you sometime. Maybe we could have dinner together, I mean just the two of us."

"I would like that. One thing I have learned about you already is that you tend to be quiet. I hope that once we get to know each other better you will be more comfortable sharing your thoughts with me."

Robert twirled the ends of the reins in his fingers before lifting his gaze to look up at Elizabeth, "You're right. I guess I tend to be more careful with my words than some people. I like to verify the facts about circumstances or other people before I say something that I don't know for sure whether it's true or not. If those facts are not clear at the time, and I share them anyway, then to me that just sounds like I'm spreading rumors. Rumors can destroy relationships."

"Wow!" Elizabeth said. "I see my comment struck hard. Maybe we could continue our conversation at a later date over dinner as you suggested."

"That would be wonderful," Robert responded.

"It's a date then." Elizabeth turned to walk away.

"Elizabeth! Thank you for visiting Susie. It really meant a lot to her and my mother."

"It was my pleasure," Elizabeth answered with a smile. She turned and walked through the front gate of the boarding house. Robert watched her until she stopped and turned to wave to him. He waved back.

—

THOMAS WRIGHT, SON OF the bank manager Theodore Wright, paid a visit to check on his friend Anna who had not fully recovered from her illness.

"I saw your boy at the bank," Thomas told Anna.

"Who are you talking about?" Anna asked.

"Robert Chambers."

"Robert! He is not my boy. What is that good for nothin' up to now?"

"I'm not sure, but I think he's been looking into buying a foreclosed farm. I'll ask my father tonight at dinner. Just so you know, I also saw him driving that new schoolteacher through town."

"Well, I see it didn't take him long to move on after dumping me like a sack of potatoes. I would like to make his life as miserable as he made mine. New schoolteacher, you say? Help me find some water to throw on his new flame."

"I have an idea," Thomas said looking at Anna who was now sitting up in bed.

"Let's hear it," Anna began coughing to the point where her breaths were labored.

"Sure you're okay?" Thomas asked.

Finally, she was able to speak again after drinking from a small cup of water on the bedside table.

Thomas took the empty glass from Anna, "I can tell my father that I have known Robert to be unstable and that he can't be trusted. With my testimony, he would surely be turned down for any kind of bank loan."

Anna raised her eyebrows and grinned, "Tell you what. Go one step further and let my daddy in on it as well. He has been friends with your father for years. He still blames

Robert for what happened to me. Didn't you say you saw Ruth Garrett in town the other day?" Anna asked hoping to enlarge the circle of conspirators.

"I did. What about it?"

"Ruth owes me a favor. She probably talks to the new schoolteacher. We can ask her to dig up some dirt on the two of them."

"That's a great idea." Thomas pulled a handkerchief from his pocket and used it to wipe the sweat off Anna's forehead. "You don't look so good, Anna. I'm concerned about you."

Her voice was weak as she coughed, "I'll be fine. You go on now. I want him to pay for the way he treated me."

Exiting the house, Thomas saw Matthew, Anna's father, in the barn and did exactly what he and Anna had planned. Later that evening, he had a similar conversation with his father during dinner.

Chapter 11

Early on Monday morning, Robert returned to town on horseback to continue his conversation with Theodore Wright.

"What do you mean the farm is no longer available?" Robert asked Theodore with a look of disbelief.

Theodore looked up peering through his monocle, "We already have a qualified buyer. Thank you for your inquiry. I will let you know if anything changes. Good day!" he stated coldly.

Robert rubbed the back of his neck unable to process what had just taken place. As far as he could tell, there had not been any issues or concerns during his previous discussions with Theodore about buying the property. Theodore had not even hinted about any other interested buyers the day before. Still, Robert was not going to give up on his dream of owning a farm, even if it meant going to a bank in a nearby town.

He remembered that Mr. Taylor had asked him to stop by the cotton broker's office in town to relay a message about upcoming shipments. He entered the open warehouse door and paused hearing a voice call out, "Can I help you?"

"I am looking for the owner, is he available?" Robert asked.

"He's not here right now. I expect him to be back in an hour. Can I give him a message?"

Robert told the man about the upcoming shipments. The worker thanked Robert for the information and assured him that he would let Simon know.

After leaving Simon's office, Robert decided to stop by the tobacco warehouse and check current tobacco prices for his father. The warehouse had just come into view when Robert looked up and saw the stocky frame of his old schoolmate Christopher Murphy walking in the direction of the tavern. Christopher was spirited and enjoyed a challenge. He was short and muscular at the age of twenty-two. Red hair and a splotchy complexion were common in his family. They were of Irish descent. Robert remembered that Christopher had frequently gotten into trouble for fighting with other boys who were normally older and taller. Robert often wondered if the gap between Christopher's front teeth was from fighting or if he was born that way. One thing he knew for sure, Christopher was always on his side, and he often kept him out of trouble. He was a dedicated friend. Christopher enlisted in the army and had just returned from Florida where he had been briefly deployed to join the fight against the Spanish in Cuba for President McKinley. Fortunately for Christopher, his company never reached foreign soil. Since his return to Petersburg, he had been living with a friend in a small house in town.

"Little early in the day for that," Robert called to Christopher before being noticed.

"It's never too early for a shot of Irish whiskey."

Robert stopped and tied the horse to the hitching post in front of the tavern. Christopher looked a little disheveled. His hat was on backward, and his clothing was wrinkled.

"You okay?" Robert asked.

Christopher looked at Robert through squinting bloodshot eyes and smiled. By the look of his red knuckles and bruised cheek, it was obvious that Christopher had been behaving like a tom cat.

"Never better!"

"How late did you stay out last night?"

"What time is it now?" Christopher asked.

"It's about ten o clock."

"What…uh, well, I guess I'm still out."

"Did you not go home again last night?"

"Let me think about that." Christopher dropped his chin into his right palm and scratched the week-old stubble before he reached up to straighten his hat. He raised his hand while pointing his finger toward the sky. "Too many questions, so few answers. I need a drink. You comin'?"

Robert had not been one to frequent the tavern, but he decided to take a few minutes to find out more about how his friend was doing. They were the only two customers in the bar that morning. They walked up to the bar. Hearing their footsteps, the bartender walked through a door from the kitchen.

"Not you again," the bartender said with a half-smile on his face. "You are becoming the best of the worst customers I have."

"I can see that you are not only ugly my friend, but you are funny as well. Pour me a shot of that Irish whiskey before I can think straight and change my mind," Christopher teased. "And don't even think about givin' me any of that local brandy everyone around here raves about."

"Whose paying' this time?" the bartender asked.

Christopher looked at Robert and slapped him on the back. "My good friend Robert here has agreed to do whatever it takes to help me become an upstanding citizen. For now, that means I need a drink."

Shaking his head, the bartender looked at Robert, "How about some coffee for you!"

"Thanks. That would be great."

They sat at the nearest table and waited until the drinks arrived. Robert told his friend how much he was enjoying his new job and about his ambition to become a cotton farmer.

"How's Susie?" Christopher asked.

Robert assured him that Susie was better and explained that she had returned to school today. He also told Christopher about the new schoolteacher in town. Robert was quite interested in Elizabeth, but he was keeping that to himself. He explained how they first met at the ferry and how he had gotten to know her better when she visited Susie.

Christopher sipped his whiskey and listened. Robert seemed to run out of words for a moment, "Elizabeth you say, a schoolteacher. Is she pretty?"

Robert looked at his friend who was squinting with

one eye partly closed, "She is a beautiful girl. Prettier than anyone I have ever seen."

"You don't say," Christopher said smiling. He lifted his glass of whiskey. "I just might have to pay her a visit."

Robert took a sip of his coffee and asked, "How about you?"

"What do you mean?" Christopher placed the glass on the table.

"Look at you. Christopher, you're my best friend. I'm just concerned. That's all."

Christopher took in a deep breath and held it for a moment. "Don't worry about me. The adjustment from being in the war has been tough; I won't lie. I thought the ship I was on would sink during one of the battles. As soon as I find a steady job I will get back on my feet." Christopher sat up in his chair and looked over his shoulder at the bartender who had once again emerged from the back. "I might even be able to work nights here at the tavern. I know most of the customers by name."

Shaking his head the bartender responded, "Yeah, and most of them are hoping to forget yours."

Robert smiled, "I will keep my eyes open and let you know if anything comes up. You might ask about work at the cotton warehouse. Our good friend John Bowman, who worked there, was recently injured. I'm sure they could use an extra hand until he gets back on his feet."

"There's not enough money in Georgia for me to work for that snake," Christopher replied looking as sober as possible.

"You mean Simon Hale?" Robert asked.

"That's him. He was in the bar not long ago with a co-worker. They were having a disagreement. I wasn't close enough to hear what was said but based on the way they looked at each other, it could not have been good. I can't put my finger on it yet, but there is something about that man that rubs me wrong."

"Well, I will help you any way I can," Robert said.

"I know you will buddy."

Robert smiled and pushed his chair back. "I have to get going." He picked up his hat from the table and twirled it by the brim.

"Watch your back!" Christopher said. "The bartender also saw the two men arguing and told me that the co-worker has not been back since."

"Thanks for the concern, but I will be fine." Robert thought about the warning his friend had given on his ride home for lunch. Simon had left both of them with a bad first impression. Robert was naturally suspicious by nature, and people had to earn his trust. He also knew that Christopher was good at reading people, and Robert trusted his judgment without question.

Robert passed the Taylor farm without stopping. He looked out at the sprawling farm and saw two rows of tenant houses on the property. It was obvious that the structures had been lived in for a long time, but they all seemed to be in good repair. Free-range chickens and dogs roamed the immediate area surrounding the houses. Children were playing in the yards while most of their parents were working in the nearby fields.

The cotton industry in Petersburg had done well largely because of the location of one of the first cotton gins in the region. The ginned cotton was transported by train or river to cotton mills in McCormick and Augusta. Even though the future of the city of Petersburg was uncertain, there was no doubt that the cotton industry was doing well.

The entire business of cotton was an eye-opening experience for Robert. He and his father had been adamant about farming tobacco, and as a result, they had both been unable to see what was right in front of them. In a twisted sort of way, he was glad that their tobacco barn had burned down. This would be the new beginning he had hoped for all these years. Even though the cotton farm he had inquired about was no longer available, he felt sure that another one would come along soon. The next time, he would be prepared to move quickly and not let another opportunity slip away.

CHAPTER 12

The cities of Vienna, South Carolina, and Lisbon, Georgia, competed with Petersburg for trade and commerce. The local train depot brought trade and visitors through the area, but few people stayed overnight since there was only one boarding house in Vienna. The train's primary function was to provide support for cotton and tobacco warehouses in the region, stopping in Vienna every morning on its way to Augusta.

The owner of the local general store opened by eight o'clock every morning to serve customers at the train depot. At times, passengers would exit the train with just enough time to grab a hot ham biscuit and hop back on before the train departed again.

Most passengers passed through Vienna on their

way to Augusta, but the few who exited were usually traveling in business coach. Vienna was the kind of town that someone needed a reason to visit.

It was Sunday morning of the following week when Simon stood at the train platform. The approaching train billowed charcoal-colored smoke from the stack as the whistle announced its arrival. After it came to a full stop, James Ridley stepped off onto the depot platform. He peered left and then right through the engulfing steam on the platform as though he was looking for something or someone.

"James!" a voice called out above the sound of the hissing engine. He turned to see Simon Hale approaching from the direction of the general store holding a small paper bag.

"Had breakfast yet?" Simon asked while handing him two ham biscuits.

"No! I'm starving."

Simon continued, "I was glad to receive your letter. You will have to tell me how you managed to escape. But first, let's get away from here before someone recognizes you."

They both needed to be careful since there were people still living in Vienna who might remember James even though he had moved away ten years earlier. The two men got in the seat of Simon's empty cotton wagon and rode off in the direction of the river.

James opened one of the bags from Simon and began eating, "Thanks, I needed this. Prison and jail food are terrible. I don't know how they call it food at all."

Turning to look at James, Simon asked, "The letter had a Milledgeville postmark. What were you doing in Milledgeville?"

James took another bite and swallowed, "Me and a buddy had been offered temporary jobs in south Georgia as foremen on a peanut farm. We were going south from Atlanta when we decided to stop overnight in Milledgeville. That night we went to the local saloon for a drink, and my friend got into a fight. He broke a whiskey bottle over some guy's head; I guess it hit him in the wrong place, 'cause the man died."

"So why were you arrested?" Simon asked.

"I had the man in a bear grip from behind when my friend hit him. Turns out he was the son of the local judge. Them boys didn't take to kindly to the killin'. We barely escaped with our lives. I thought they were going to lynch us before they could get us to jail."

Simon pulled on his hat and his eyebrows wrinkled. He turned to James and asked, "So how did you manage to escape?"

"We had been in jail for nearly a month. The local judge wasn't allowed to sentence us since we killed his son, so they were waiting for a judge from another town. I noticed prisoners were being moved in and out of jail. I talked with one of them one night, and he said that there was a local hospital, a crazy house, where they treat sick prisoners. I came up with a plan for my friend to start acting out of his head. For over a week he whooped and hollered, climbed the jail cell, and made life miserable for almost everybody there including the sheriff. One morning I asked him to take one of the tin coffee cups and hit me in the face as hard as he could. Didn't think he would turn the cup handle towards me. That's how I got this nasty scar on my cheek. With me bleeding all over the place and my friend jumping up and down over my outstretched body, I guess they couldn't take no more. They carted both of us off to the hospital, bound in chains. We stayed there about two months before we were able to overpower a guard when he came in to deliver us a new set of prison clothes."

"You are crazier than I thought. Hit in the face with a tin cup? I would like to say that's the dumbest thing I ever heard of, but look at you, here you are," Simon laughed noticing the long scar on James' cheek.

Simon and James first met in Atlanta. In those days,

James functioned more as a bodyguard for Simon than a sidekick or business associate. James had come to Simon's defense on more than one occasion. Most of the time it involved the consumption of alcohol mixed with a high-stakes game of poker. Simon had almost gotten them both killed late one night at a saloon in south Atlanta.

About a mile from the river, they turned down a narrow, seldom-used roadbed. At the end of the overgrown wagon ruts, was an old tenant house that had been abandoned for months.

Simon stopped just in front of the tenant house, "You can stay here for now."

"Are you sure this is a good idea? This place looks terrible. How do I know it won't fall in on me while I'm sleeping?" James questioned.

Simon had evicted the last tenants. The one-room shack was not much to look at, but it had been much worse before Simon forced a worker to scrub the place from top to bottom. He also filled the pantry with enough canned goods to last a few weeks.

Simon answered, "It's suitable enough. It might leak a bit if it rains, but those timbers will still be standing years from now."

Once inside, Simon squinted with a half-smile, "I have been able to encourage some of the locals to get out of the tobacco business, but we have made a few mistakes. Did you get my last letter before going south?"

"You mean the letter about Thomas?"

"Yes. Thomas made a critical mistake by being seen arguing with a farmer's son whose body was found in the ashes of their torched tobacco barn a week later. Not only that, but a temporary worker recently stumbled on one of our moonshine shipments hidden in a cotton wagon. Our attempt to silence him failed."

"You must be kidding!" James barked. "Simon, I did not come back here to get arrested and sent back to prison. I can't go back there. How in the hell…"

"Stop!" Simon shouted. "It's all been taken care of, but we must be careful. I'm glad you're here."

Simon explained that this would be the place that they would meet from now on. He suggested that they try to not be seen together. James had been run out of Vienna once, and there was an extensive line of unpleasant characters who would be eager to get even with him if they knew he was back in town.

"Get settled in here and I will stop by tomorrow to discuss my plan to close down another tobacco farm. It won't be long until most everyone around here is out of the tobacco business," Simon said with a laugh. His plan was to eliminate as many tobacco farmers as possible and purchase their land at foreclosure auctions. By doing so, he could also convert the farms to growing cotton which supplemented his business as a cotton broker. Adding to his profits, Simon was also making money from the sale of moonshine in the area. He was becoming not only greedy but dangerous. Now that he and James were working together again, he was planning to become even more aggressive in claiming more land for pennies on the dollar.

"James my boy, we are both going to be very wealthy one day," Simon said putting a log on the fire and stoking the dying flame with a poker.

"I can almost smell the money now," James added with a laugh while focusing on the flame. "Should we be worried about someone seeing smoke from the chimney?"

"The house is far enough off the road that I don't think anyone passing by would even notice," Simon answered. "No one knows you're here, and we need to keep it that way. Anyway, even if someone did notice a sign of life here, they would just think that it was still occupied by the farm workers who were living here before. Try and get some rest; we have a lot of planning to do, and I need to tell you more about some of the people that will be involved." Simon pointed to the chest of drawers, "I left you a change of clothes in the chest. They should just about be your size."

"Thanks! I'll be needing those," James replied.

The fire had grown from embers to flames lighting the interior of the old house. Furnishings were sparse, but the bare necessities were there: a table, a bed, a chest of drawers, and a cast iron stove used for cooking.

James continued, "I suppose this will be fine for now. I'd like to build a nice new home for myself with some of the money we make."

"By the time we are done, you could own the entire town of Petersburg if you wanted," Simon said spreading his arms in front of him. "But, that's enough for now. We can talk later. I have to get back to Petersburg. I am having dinner tonight with an eligible young lady."

CHAPTER 13

It was a short ride from Simon's home to the boarding house. He had spent several hours that afternoon preparing for their evening together. Elizabeth was hesitant to accept an invitation to visit a man's home for dinner, but there were no alternatives unless they ate at the boarding house or the tavern. Neither of those would have allowed for any privacy. She found some level of comfort knowing that his home was not far from his neighbors, some of whom she had met. She reluctantly accepted on the condition that the house would be well-lit, windows left uncovered, and that Simon would take her back to the boarding house immediately following dinner.

The weather was perfect for a late afternoon carriage ride. Simon drove slowly so they could enjoy a pleasant conversation. The October sunset illuminated the sky with spectacular rays of orange and yellow streaks. It seemed to be on fire as the sun pushed beams of light that looked like they stretched to the top of the world. There was still a few minutes before dark. Simon drove the carriage to the top of a small hill where they could see the winding river that stretched out before them. He turned in a westward direction and stopped. They both sat in silence for a moment taking in the artwork of God that was on full display before them.

Elizabeth said, "This view is amazing. I can't remember when I have seen a more beautiful sunset."

"I agree," Simon answered. "I have forgotten how beautiful nature can be. We should take more time to admire God's creation. Did you say that your father is a minister?"

"Yes! He has served as pastor of the same congregation back home since I was a little girl." She turned to Simon, "Do you attend church?"

Simon replied, "To be honest, I have not been in church since moving here. My mother used to attend a Methodist church when we lived in Atlanta."

"Then you should plan to come with me sometime. There is a small Methodist congregation here in town.

Kate Norman has invited me to come with her. You could join us."

"That's a thought. Can you see the top of that home on the far ridge?" Simon asked while pointing off in the distance.

"Yes, I think so."

"I recently purchased that property. The house isn't much to look at, but the fields are perfect for growing cotton."

Elizabeth asked, "So, was that a yes?"

"I'm sorry, what was the question?"

"Yes, that you will go to church with me."

"We shall see. Let's talk about that the next time we are together."

To Elizabeth, it sounded as though Simon was not interested in church. Church worship and fellowship had been an important part of her life, and she was hesitant to become romantically involved with anyone who did not attend church. She had seen many women in her father's church whose husbands never attended. It made her sad to think of becoming a church widow. She knew that was a harsh interpretation of those women's circumstances, but church attendance was a critical component of her life, and she could not imagine a future with a husband who opted out of church. In her mind, she would just as soon remain single as to marry someone who did not share her beliefs.

The brilliant colors of the sky gave way to darker shades of gray and blue. Simon looked at Elizabeth, "Are you ready for dinner?"

"That sounds wonderful! Thank you for bringing me here to enjoy this gorgeous view."

After arriving at the house, Simon came around the carriage and extended his hand up to Elizabeth. She grasped his hand and stepped to the ground.

"Thank you," she said.

"Please come in," Simon said motioning in the direction of the front door.

"Your home looks very nice."

"I'm glad you like it. It has been quite a project. You should have seen it when I first moved in. I paid to have the complete inside cleaned and repainted. Most of the furnishings are new as well."

Simon reached around her to turn the doorknob. His arm gently brushed against her shoulder before he stepped back allowing Elizabeth to enter first.

"Your home looks amazing."

"Please come in," Simon replied.

The table was beautifully decorated with a white

tablecloth, China dishes, silverware, and fresh-cut flowers in a vase.

"Oh my! Simon, what a wonderful treat."

"I cut some of those wildflowers myself," he said. "Please have a seat." Simon moved behind Elizabeth and slid a chair back from the table inviting her to sit. After sliding her chair forward, he took his own seat.

Most of their conversation at dinner was about their careers. Elizabeth told Simon about her family and wanted to hear about his, but he seemed more interested in talking about business. The only thing she had learned about his family was that they lived in Atlanta, and Simon was an only child.

It had been a long time since Elizabeth had been out to dinner with a suitor. Caring for her mother while finishing college had taken all of her energy leaving little time for social interactions. Now that she was teaching, her spare time was consumed by grading papers and creating lesson plans. Being a new teacher was taking up more of her day than she ever imagined it would.

"That was delicious," Elizabeth spoke while moving a cloth napkin from her lap to the table.

"I'm glad you enjoyed it," Simon answered. "Annie comes over occasionally to prepare special meals. Her cornbread is the best I have ever tasted." Annie was a negro whose husband, Willie, occasionally helped with outside chores while Annie helped to clean and cook for Simon.

"I will have to meet her and ask for the recipe. The potatoes seemed to have been cooked in the juices of the beef, and that strawberry cake she made was wonderful."

"She's as good as gold," Simon said while moving his napkin from his lap to the table. "Would you sit for a few more minutes before I take you home?"

Elizabeth hesitated. The offer sounded both inviting and concerning. She barely knew this man, and now she was alone with him. His intentions seemed innocent, and she had not felt uncomfortable or nervous for a single moment that they had been together. She wondered if her uneasiness was because she had not been in a relationship for a long time and was uncomfortable with the situation, not necessarily Simon.

"I guess we can take a few minutes to sit if you wish," she replied. "Can I help with the dishes?"

"Oh no. Just leave them for now. I will clean them up later or leave them for Annie who will be here in the morning."

"Let's move to the main living area," Simon stood and walked over to pull Elizabeth's chair out from the table.

"Thank you," she said.

They walked into a spacious room in the front of the

house. "Have a seat here on the sofa if you like," Simon offered. Elizabeth sat first, then Simon sat allowing for a comfortable space between them. "Are you sure you are comfortable here?" Simon asked reassuringly. "If you prefer, I could move over to the chair next to the sofa."

"No, this will be fine," Elizabeth answered glancing in the direction of the chair and then back at Simon.

Simon turned to look at her, "Life is filled with wonderful surprises. It isn't often that such a beautiful and graceful young lady as you moves to Petersburg. And now, here we sit after enjoying a wonderful meal together. Even though I had not seen you up close until the other day at the Bowman's home, I had been hearing rumors about your exquisite charm, grace, and beauty. Now I know that the rumors are true."

"You are too kind, Simon. You seem to have thought of everything, even those," Elizabeth said pointing to a table that held another magnificent bouquet of fresh-cut flowers.

"Fresh flowers are hard to find here. In preparation for this dinner, I sent a request by a friend who happened to be going to Lincolnton to pick those up for me."

"How nice! They are beautiful," Elizabeth said. "I see you have a piano. Do you play?"

"Watch," Simon rose from the sofa, walked over to the piano, sat on the bench, and began using his feet to pump two pedals at the base. The room was immediately filled with a spirited and joyful melody.

"That sounds wonderful. What song is that?" Elizabeth asked trying to speak above the sound that reverberated off the ceiling.

"My newest song roll and my favorite by the way. The tune is titled *Just One Girl*," Simon answered.

"That makes me want to dance," Elizabeth said. "I haven't danced in years."

"You go right ahead. I would step in and lead, but as soon as I take my feet off these pedals, the music will stop."

Elizabeth giggled and twirled around like a schoolgirl while Simon happily pumped and watched. He began clapping his hands to the rhythm of the music. When the song concluded, Elizabeth made a grand pirouette. She was breathless by the end and filled with a joy she had not felt for a long time.

Simon rose from the piano stool and instinctively applauded and then reached around Elizabeth who was laughing hysterically. Realizing the transition, Elizabeth softly pushed away, "Oh Simon! That was more wonderful than you could ever know. Next time let's get Annie or another friend to join us. They can pump the organ while the two of us dance together."

"I would like that very much," Simon concluded.

"So that sounds like a commitment for another date in the future."

"I wouldn't miss it. I enjoyed the evening, Simon, but it's getting late. I really must go."

Simon glanced at his gold pocket watch, "Certainly. Let's go."

He retrieved her shawl and gently wrapped it around her shoulders. They walked out to the waiting carriage and drove away in the direction of the boarding house.

———

"WELL, I WANT TO hear all about it," Ruth demanded excitedly. She had been waiting at the boarding house dinner table for Elizabeth to return. Elizabeth did not know that Ruth had also enjoyed dinner with Simon on multiple occasions. She, however, had no intentions of telling Elizabeth.

"He was a perfect gentleman. I made several requests before accepting the invitation, and he met every one of them."

"Oh, look at you. You're blushing. Will you see him again?" she asked with forced enthusiasm.

"Of course. We have already started to plan our next visit."

"How does he compare to Robert?"

"Ruth, please! Where are you going with this?"

"I don't mean to sound too personal or anything like that. It's just that I'm curious. After all, there aren't too many eligible bachelors around here."

"Well, they both act like gentlemen. Like each of us, they have strengths and weaknesses. Robert is kind but is preoccupied with establishing his business again. Simon seems more interested in business than anything else, and yet he is more attentive than Robert."

Ruth did not share her interest in Robert or her experience with Simon. Elizabeth retired to bed naïve about her friend's underlying intentions.

CHAPTER 14

The next afternoon, Simon rode to the boarding house to invite Elizabeth to join him again for dinner. When he arrived, Ruth was sitting in a rocking chair on the front porch. Simon drew a deep breath and walked in her direction.

"How's your love life?" she asked with a smirk. She looked up at Simon and continued to rock slowly back and forth in the chair.

"Why do you care?" Simon objected. He was in no mood to tolerate Ruth's sarcasm.

She continued, "I'd say you're a day late and a dollar short. Don't waste your time on Elizabeth. She's taken a liking to Robert Chambers."

"You mean the son of the ferryman?"

"That's him!"

"He's of no consequence, just like you," Simon blurted.

"Why Simon, you flatter me. You might want to hear what I have to say. Elizabeth told me that Robert is on to you and your little undercover business activities."

"What!" Simon snapped. His eyes bore down on Ruth. "That's impossible."

"Don't get short with me. I'm only trying to help you. Elizabeth told me that Robert saw you drinking from what looked like a jar of moonshine the other night at the tavern. Robert thinks you're a distributor."

"That's a lie," Simon retorted sharply.

"Why Simon, it would be a tragedy for such a fine upstanding member of our community to be caught selling illegal moonshine in the county. Since we're such good friends and all, I thought you might like it if I dug up some dirt on Robert for you. You know what I mean, just enough to cause a rift in his relationship with Elizabeth. There's no telling what I might learn."

"Go on," Simon encouraged.

"Anyway, I would like nothing better than to get thick with Robert Chambers. Once I whisper sweet little nothings in his ear. Why, I could shuck him like a late-season ear of corn."

"You must be crazy. What makes you think I need your help?"

"It would be a downright shame if word got out about what really happened to that poor man who was crushed by one of your cotton wagons. Why I declare, information as valuable as that might be worth a little somethin' if you know what I mean. But anyway, why should I care."

Simon's nostrils flared; his eyes narrowed as he moved within inches of her face. "If you think you can blackmail me, you have underestimated who you're dealing with."

"Oh, I know who I am dealing with," Ruth said with a look of assurance as she rolled her eyes. "I'll tell you one final time. Either cut me in on the deal, or I will present evidence that will expose the real reason why you're in Petersburg."

Exasperated Simon spouted, "See what you can get out of Robert. But I'm warning you, if you mess this up, your life in this little town will be miserable."

"Why Simon, you have such a way with words, you sly devil you. You go on now so I can get busy. This undercover work is exhausting," Ruth laughed mockingly. "Your sweet Elizabeth is not here anyway."

Simon did not trust Ruth. He was not convinced that Robert knew anything about his bootleg business, but with all the problems he had faced recently, he could not take a chance. He knew that Robert did not have enough evidence even if someone did see him drinking moonshine, besides, the local sheriff would not be interested in acting on the information.

Simon knew how conniving Ruth could be. He continued, "I like your idea of getting information that I can use to discredit Robert. I'm working hard to establish a relationship with Elizabeth, and the last thing I need is for that farmer boy to get in my way."

Ruth looked up at Simon, "That hurts me to the core Simon. I just knew that you and I were going to be spending more time together. Now you are courting yet another young woman. It just leaves me heartsick." Ruth began to laugh. Simon turned in disgust and walked away.

"I will be happy to help you. Bye, sugar!" Ruth called out sarcastically as Simon walked through the gate and slammed it shut with such force that the fence rattled.

"What are you helping Simon do?" Kate Norman questioned walking onto the porch.

"Oh, hello, Kate," Ruth said startled but trying to regain her composure. "Simon asked if I could come by his office in the next few days and help him with his bookkeeping. He knows I teach and thought I could help him get caught up."

"I see. I'm sure that he is a busy man. I hear that he has begun to purchase a lot of farms around here. I just can't imagine how someone could have that much money."

Ruth responded, "Simon has learned how to leverage credit. Most of the farms he purchased were bought using money from loans."

"He must be on good terms with the bank manager. I was turned down just a few months ago when I applied for a small loan to help me repaint the exterior of the boarding house."

"I guess there is just not enough money to go around," Ruth countered while getting up from her chair. "Please pardon me, Mrs. Norman, but I need to go upstairs and freshen up. I plan to walk to the livery stable and hire a carriage for a short ride."

"Where are you headed?" Kate asked.

"Nowhere in particular. I just need some fresh air and new scenery."

"That sounds wonderful. I hope you find both." Kate responded.

———

RUTH HIRED A CARRIAGE to transport her to the Chamber's home. Upon arrival, she found Robert outside splitting firewood.

"Well, hello there handsome," she called from the carriage which had rolled to a stop.

Robert had seen the carriage approaching, but since the house was not far off the main road, he assumed it was headed for the ferry. Hearing a familiar voice, he spun around.

"Ruth, what are you doing here? Do you need to cross the river?"

Ruth stepped out of the carriage and walked over to Robert. His chest was rising and falling as perspiration dripped from his chin. "By no means! I came here to see you. I want to know why you never came to call on me again. It just wasn't right for you to break off our relationship so suddenly. What did I do?"

"Ruth, please. We never had a relationship, and I never called on you. It was you who came here to meet Susie."

Ruth began visiting the Chamber's home as soon as she heard about Robert. She visited on the pretense of meeting Susie; however, Robert was her real interest. Her unwanted advances had been an offense to Robert at the time, and he had made that clear to Ruth.

"Of course, I know that, silly. But it's not every day that I have the opportunity to spend time with such a fine strapping young man such as yourself. First come, first served, as they say."

"Why are you here?"

"Don't get huffy. I heard that you were in the market for a new love now that Anna has moved on, so I thought this would be a good chance for us to get reacquainted."

"What makes you think I am interested in a relationship?"

"Well, you know that Elizabeth Bright and I live together at the boarding house. She just goes on and on about how kind and handsome you are. I think she is in love with you. But she's not right for you, Robert. How about we rekindle our old flame?"

Robert's jaw tightened, "I admit that Elizabeth and I met when she came to visit Susie, but I have no intentions of being in a relationship with anyone. I'm sorry you wasted your time and your money on the carriage ride." Robert lifted the ax signaling that the conversation was over.

"Now then, I can sure understand why you would be upset. I mean with the word getting out around town about you and Anna losing that baby and all," Ruth taunted and waited for his reaction. He did not disappoint.

"What!" Robert answered dropping the ax on the ground.

"My, that does seem to be a touchy subject, doesn't it?"

"That's a lie, and you know it." Robert stepped closer speaking with quiet intensity.

Ruth continued, "Anyway, I will let you think about my offer for a while. Oh, by the way, Elizabeth told me that you were not fond of her latest suitor. I think that she and Simon are a perfect match. Sounds to me like you are a little jealous of his success and charm. She also said something about some problems related to Simon drinking moonshine. For the life of me, I can't imagine why that's important. Do you?"

Robert's face turned red, "Please leave!"

"If you insist," Ruth stared but did not move.

"Now!" Robert shouted.

"Your loss, but I'll be back another time. Maybe next time you won't have such a bad attitude. Bye, for now." Ruth turned and walked back to the waiting carriage. After she got in, the driver turned towards town.

Robert's head was spinning. He was not sure whom he detested the most right now, Anna or Ruth. Each of them had made his life miserable. His first thought was to turn away from any relationship, including one with Elizabeth even though he was extremely fond of her. She was the first woman he had met who seemed like a genuinely good person.

Robert hated conflict. He did not run from it when

given no alternative, but it was easier to just ignore some problems and wish them away. This was one of those times when he knew that ignoring the problem would only make matters worse. He decided that it was time to tell his parents everything he knew about Anna, her relationship with Thomas, and his knowledge of the pregnancy.

"Robert!" his mother called from the porch. "Dinner is ready."

Chapter 15

The following Saturday could not have come soon enough for Elizabeth. She needed a well-deserved break from school. Her plan for today was to prepare a picnic lunch and walk to a familiar bluff that allowed her the best vantage point to enjoy the cool October air, the beautiful fall leaves, and the peacefulness of the river. Mrs. Norman helped her with lunch and even provided a basket to carry the sandwich and fruit. Fall was Elizabeth's favorite time of year. Upon arrival at the bluff, she spread a blanket in the open field. The sun warmed her body while she sat watching the tops of wildflowers and uncut hay sway to the rhythm of a gentle breeze. It was a perfect day. She looked up at the lacy-edged granite-colored clouds and traced the outlines of imaginary figures. One cloud formed the shape of a dog's face, another the side profile of a person wearing a hat.

Elizabeth reclined on the blanket and closed her eyes. She thought about her father and prayed that he was well and not working too hard. She desperately missed her father and was beginning to make plans to see him over the holidays. She also thought about her mother and the circumstances that brought her to Petersburg. She must have been lying on the blanket for a long time when she heard the grass rustling behind her. She sat up and saw Simon approaching.

"Mind if I join you?" he asked. "I saw you walking in this direction. I would have come up right away but figured you might need some alone time."

"Hello, Simon! Please have a seat." Simon did as she asked and sat on the edge of the blanket as Elizabeth made room for him.

"You're right. Teaching children can be exhausting. I would offer you some lunch, but I only planned for one."

"That's kind of you, but I can't stay. I just wanted to say hello and to thank you again for having dinner with me. I hope that we can enjoy another meal together soon."

"Yes, let's do!" Elizabeth responded.

"How do you like Petersburg?" Simon asked looking over his shoulder in the direction of town.

"I enjoy my students, and Mrs. Norman at the boarding house is nice," she paused.

"But…," Simon added and waited for her response.

"Well, I miss my family. This is the first time in my life to live away from home, and it has proved to be more difficult than I thought."

"I can understand that," Simon responded. "I have not seen my family in Atlanta since moving here over a year ago."

"I'm glad you understand," she said.

Simon leaned back supporting himself with his arms and removed his hat. He looked up at the trees as a gentle breeze caused the tree limbs to dance in the wind. "I feel so at home when I am with you. It's hard to explain. I'm not sure I have ever felt this way about someone whom I have known for such a short time."

Elizabeth blushed, "To tell you the truth, I was just thinking the same thing about you. We just met one another, but yet I am remarkably comfortable in your presence."

Simon sat back up and reached over taking Elizabeth by the hand, "I wish I could spend the day here with you, but unfortunately, I must be off. I'm on my way to another business deal. This one is near Vienna. I hope to see you again soon." Simon stood, "Enjoy your day. I'll see you soon."

"Are you sure you can't stay a while?" Elizabeth asked looking up at Simon.

"Quite sure," he replied.

"Well, then, I look forward to our next meal together," she said.

He bid Elizabeth goodbye, then turned and walked down the hill a short distance to where his horse was tied to a tree and grazing.

Elizabeth watched Simon ride away leaving her feeling excited and nervous. She was quite attracted to him, but she had not courted in a long time. There was also the issue of establishing a serious relationship this far away from home. It was still too soon for her to know if Petersburg would become her permanent home. The stories about the city being in decline were evident. The uncertainty of it all made her feel anxious, but at least for today, she pushed away her insecurities and enjoyed the beautiful day.

———

AT MID-MORNING, ROBERT RODE his horse into town to visit his friend Christopher. He had not gone far when he happened to look over his shoulder and saw a large plume of smoke in the sky. He turned around and rode back towards the ferry. When Robert reached the river, he met his father returning from the other side.

"What's the hurry?" William asked.

"You can't see it from here, but there is smoke coming from the direction of Vienna. I thought I would ride over to be sure it's not one of Mr. Taylor's farms."

When the ferry landed on the Carolina shore, he told his father that he would be back soon. Nearing Vienna, he could see that the smoke trail grew, and in the distance, a tobacco barn was visible with flames shooting through the roof. Close by was a farmhouse and another barn which would have housed the animals and hay.

With no one in sight, he pulled up and tied his horse to a hitching post in front of the farmhouse. Memories flooded his mind. This barn was similar to the one he and his father once owned. The fire was raging and would be impossible to put out. Robert thought that it seemed odd for this fire to be burning and yet no one was around. He walked onto the porch of the house and knocked. When no one responded, he walked around the farmhouse. Seeing no one, he entered the animal barn and found a horse in its stall and a saddle hanging on the top of a fence rail, evidence that the owner was still around.

Just then, he heard the rumble of several horses

galloping in his direction. As he exited the barn, one of the riders drew his gun from its holster, pointed it at Robert, and shouted, "Get your hands up. What were you doing in there?"

Robert held up his hands. "I just rode up same as you. I saw the smoke from the other side of the river. I work for Mr. Fred Taylor and was afraid one of his farms might be burning."

"Why were you in the barn?" the man continued with his gun still trained on Robert.

"I told you that I just arrived and decided to see if someone was on the property," Robert said.

With the galloping sound of hooves, the men turned to see Sheriff Joseph Davidson approaching. Looking at the three men and then back at Robert, Joseph said, "I was on my way to Petersburg when I saw the smoke. Robert, what are you doing here?"

Robert recounted the same story to Joseph that he told the other three men.

Joseph looked at the man holding the gun, "Holster your gun. Robert's a friend of mine."

The man followed the sheriff's order, and all four men dismounted.

"This is Jerry's farm," one of the men said. Looking at Robert he asked, "Have you seen him?"

"I don't know Jerry, but I checked around the house before coming into the barn."

"You went into the house?" another man questioned.

"No! I knocked and called out, but no one answered."

They all walked onto the front porch of the house. The door was unlocked. Joseph slowly pushed the door open and walked in with the other men close behind. "Jerry," he called out as the door creaked fully open. They walked through the main entrance of a small two-room farmhouse towards a partly open door that led to the bedroom. "Jerry," Joseph called again loudly pushing the door fully open while holding his revolver in the other hand.

A large man lay face down on the floor in a pool of blood. The sheriff rolled him over revealing multiple stab wounds. From the overturned furniture, it appeared a struggle had occurred.

"Where is Jer…," a man's voice trailed off seeing the body of his friend. "Oh, my God! What happened?"

"A vicious stabbing," Joseph answered.

They began to search for evidence of the offender and his motive. Robbery did not seem to be the intent because nothing outside of the bedroom had been disturbed. Two of the men grabbed under each of Jerry's arms and drug his body outside.

One of Jerry's friends said, "There had to be more

than one person involved with this. I've known Jerry for a long time. He was big and strong as an ox. It would be impossible for one man to attack him and get away without being injured or killed."

"Where is his family?" Robert asked.

"He don't have any family," the friend answered. "He's lived alone for over ten years."

"Why would someone want to kill him?" Sheriff Davidson asked.

"It don't make sense. Jerry was a kind soul. Wouldn't hurt a fly. He mostly stayed to himself. The last time I saw him was about two weeks ago. He was telling me about some stranger who stopped by and tried to convince him to grow cotton instead of tobacco. Jerry was mad as a hornet. He'd farmed tobacco his whole life and made a decent living."

Hearing that comment made Robert shiver. How could it be that this same story seemed to be replaying over and over? It was obvious that cotton growers were increasing, but he never considered that someone might be pressuring others to switch from tobacco to cotton. But what would be the purpose of that? Making a quick connection, Robert remembered that Simon had only recently begun ginning and warehousing cotton. The previous owners of the cotton gin had suffered a death in the family followed by financial troubles, which caused them to close their business. Simon had purchased everything from the family soon after.

It still did not make sense to Robert. He understood that more cotton growers would equate to more revenue from the cotton industry for a local cotton broker like Simon, but why would anyone resort to violence, even murder, to accomplish that? Questions flooded his mind. Even if someone was threatening farmers to switch from tobacco to cotton, why would they go to the trouble of destroying a current tobacco crop by fire? Robert was fully convinced that their tobacco barn fire was not an accident. Could the same person or persons be intentionally setting these fires, and if so, why?

Robert's thoughts were interrupted when Joseph asked, "Did Jerry tell you what the man looked like?"

"He never said any more to me about it," the friend answered.

Joseph looked at the men. "Why don't you see if there's a wagon in the barn. Load his body in it and take it to the undertaker in Parksville." After the men departed, Joseph and Robert remained inside searching for clues.

"I don't understand," Joseph said. "If robbery was a motive, then normally the drawer contents would have been strewn about. Every drawer so far looks like things are just as Jerry would have left them. Let's have a look around outside."

By now the burning barn had been reduced to smoldering ash and smoke.

Robert spoke, "Joseph, I have an ominous feeling about this cotton-loving visitor. What would be his motive for trying to convince Jerry to grow cotton? Why would anyone kill what we believe to be an innocent man and then burn his tobacco barn?"

Joseph pulled on the front of his hat, "I was just thinking the same thing. I don't have any evidence, except for Jerry's body, to help me come up with a motive. What if Jerry had enemies from some relationship or failed business adventure? We just don't know enough yet to be sure of anything."

The two men walked around the ruined structure looking for evidence. Joseph found a set of large footprints in the area of the tobacco barn and called Robert over to inspect the prints.

"This looks like the same size footprint that I found behind our barn," Robert explained as he walked up beside Joseph and looked down at the hard-packed clay.

"That would be hard to prove since Jerry's foot is about the same size," Joseph responded.

Robert continued walking around the barn stopping

to look at the ashes where the barn door once stood. He caught a glimpse of something small that looked like a chain. It was too shiny to be an old door hinge. Pushing back some of the ash with his boot, he uncovered a gold pocket watch. He kicked the watch away from the hot ashes and used a glove to pick it up. There weren't many tobacco farmers who would have been so extravagant to own a nice gold watch like this one. He managed to open the face of the watch while calling Joseph to come and look. There were three initials engraved on the inside cover,

S. E. H.

CHAPTER 16

It was about noon when Robert arrived back in Petersburg after stopping long enough to tell his father about the fire and murder. William was visibly shaken by the news of Jerry's death, "I remember meeting Jerry about twelve years ago at a tobacco auction in McCormick. He was a nice man. I remember he told me that his wife was sick, and the doctors hadn't been much help. They didn't have children or any other family in the area."

Robert responded, "A group of Jerry's friends came by while I was there, and one of them told me that Jerry's wife died about ten years ago."

"That is such a shame."

"Yes, it is."

William continued, "I can't understand why so many

tobacco barns have burned recently, including our own. Why I can't remember a single other tobacco barn fire in the last ten years except these."

"Have you had many people riding the ferry this morning?" Robert asked.

"Saturday is one of my busiest days. I'd say there have been thirty or more people going back and forth this mornin'."

"Do you remember Simon Hale? We met him on the road several months ago."

"Why yes! He has been crossing more often lately. I took him across early this morning."

Robert did not tell his father about the pocket watch. He felt sure Simon had been there; however, a gold watch was not enough evidence to convict him.

He wanted to go straight to Simon and question him about the watch, but the Sheriff discouraged it. If he went directly to Simon, then he might try to claim that he lost it earlier and was thankful to them for finding it. Joseph preferred to hang on to the watch and bring it forth as evidence at the appropriate time allowing him more time to investigate the crime.

"I'm going to head into town," Robert said. I was on my way to visit Christopher when I saw the smoke."

"Why don't you stop by the house and get a bite to

eat? I told your ma that you crossed in a hurry. She was worried that something was wrong."

"I have worked up an appetite. Lunch sounds good."

Robert's mother had just made fresh cornbread and turnip greens. The smell permeated the house. Martha was at the stove frying chicken, and Susie was getting out plates and glasses as the two men walked in. A large container of sweet tea was in the middle of the table. Martha had made peach cobbler earlier that morning. Although times were hard, the family continued to share an ample lunch together each Saturday.

Susie spoke first, "Come in and eat with us."

"Don't mind if I do," Robert responded pulling back a chair. Surveying the table he said, "This looks amazing."

Martha teased, "It's nothing really. Just a little something I threw together."

"Your father told me you crossed the river in a big hurry this morning. What was that all about?" Martha asked pulling the last piece of chicken out of the black skillet.

"I just saw a lot of smoke in the distance and was worried about one of Mr. Taylor's farms, so I went to take a look."

"Is everything all right?"

"Is everything all right with what?" William asked as he grabbed his wife playfully from behind.

"I'm not talking to you, old man," she laughed.

"Who are you calling old? If that ain't the pot calling the kettle black," William cajoled. They both laughed out loud.

Susie and Robert looked at each other while the friendly banter between their parents continued.

"You're the worst wife I have," William said with a big grin.

"I'm the only wife you have, you old cuss unless you're not telling me something."

"Lord help, I have enough trouble providing for the one I have. I never did understand those Bible stories where men had all those wives and such."

Laughter erupted as the family took their place at the table. Martha cut her eyes at William playfully.

The special Saturday meal had become one of the family's best traditions, and everyone looked forward to that time together. Knowing the tradition's importance, William had found an assistant to help on the weekends, since the ferry was busy most every Saturday. William raised his hands and asked the family to stop passing food and to bow with him. During his prayer, William asked God to bless the ferry owner and his family. Although the job did not pay much, William knew that it came during a time of desperate need. They were all grateful that the job provided an opportunity to put food on the table and a roof over their heads.

While they continued to pass bowls of food, Susie looked at Robert and blurted out, "Miss Garrett said that you were in love."

Robert's face turned red causing him to choke on a bite of fried chicken, "She what?" he said reaching for his glass of tea.

"She told me that you and Miss Bright are in love."

"Now, now Susie. We told you not to spread rumors. That is a rumor, isn't it Robert?" Martha asked with a slight grin.

"Mother! Of course, it's a rumor. I can't deny that I am fond of Elizabeth Bright, but to say that we are in love is just not right."

"Well, even if it isn't a rumor, that would be all right with me," Martha added.

"Me too," William said.

Susie laughed aloud, "See, I was right!"

"Alright now, that's enough Susie," Martha continued. "Let Robert finish his meal so he can get on about his business."

After the meal, Susie helped her mother clean and put away the dishes. William walked back to the ferry and Robert rode into town to Christopher's home.

"Just landed my dream job," Christopher grinned looking at Robert who walked in the door and sat beside him at the table.

"Yea! What's that?" Robert asked.

"I'm the new nighttime barkeep at the tavern. The money's not great, but I get all the food and drink I want."

"Knowing you, it wouldn't surprise me if you don't owe the tavern owner money by the end of the night," Robert said with a smile.

"No problem there. The owner told me that business had increased since I started."

"Congratulations!"

"Thanks, Robert. There is one thing though that troubles me."

"What's that? Robert asked.

"The owner told me that someone is selling moonshine in the community, and he wants to know who it is. It's bad for business."

"I've been hearing about the moonshine from my friend Joseph," Robert said.

"You mean Sheriff Joseph Davidson from Parksville?"

"Yes. He's a good friend."

Christopher leaned in with a hushed tone, "I have to tell you this. The other night I saw Simon Hale pull a small mason jar from his overcoat pocket and pour it in his glass and the glass of a stranger sitting with him."

"What'd the man look like?" Robert asked.

"Big man with a long scar on his cheek. Burly sort of fella. Walked with a limp."

Suddenly, the front door opened, and a man entered.

"Hey, Mac!" Christopher greeted the guest, "This is my friend Robert."

"Call me Mac," the man said while reaching for Robert's hand.

"We were just talking about your favorite subject Mac," Christopher said.

"What's that?" Mac asked.

"Moonshine." Christopher continued.

Mac shrugged letting out a forced laugh, "You got me there."

"Mac sure likes his moonshine. That is, whenever he can find it," Christopher added.

The three men continued their conversation about the possible sources for the influx of moonshine from South Carolina. During their conversation, Simon's name was mentioned. Mac told them that he had been working for a cotton farmer and had seen Simon around the farm on a couple of occasions.

"Why do you think Simon was at your employer's farm?" Robert asked Mac.

Mac answered, "I didn't think much about it, after all, he is the cotton broker. It wouldn't be that unusual for him to stop by and check on any upcoming shipments."

"I guess that's true," Robert said.

Mac offered, "I do have to say though that there is something shady about him. It's hard to explain."

"You don't have to explain that to us," Christopher responded.

They all agreed that Simon made them uneasy. Christopher offered to keep an eye out at the tavern for any suspicious activity.

After leaving Christopher's home, Robert decided to visit Elizabeth. It was time to share his concerns about Simon with her. Elizabeth had just returned from her picnic and was putting away Kate's basket when she heard a light tapping on the frame of the kitchen door.

"Robert!" Elizabeth gasped and turned suddenly. "You scared me. I didn't hear you come in."

"I didn't mean to startle you. I was wondering if you would have dinner with me at the tavern tonight?"

"Is there something on your mind?" Elizabeth's brow furrowed.

"Can we talk about it at dinner?" Robert asked.

"I guess so if you are sure everything is all right. Is Susie ill again?"

"Oh no! Susie is fine. I was just hoping we could spend some time together. You know, get to know one another better."

Elizabeth glanced at the pendulum clock on the kitchen wall, "How does five o clock sound?"

"Perfect! I will meet you here, and we can walk to the tavern."

"Good! See you then," Elizabeth answered.

Although Robert was concerned about Elizabeth's relationship with Simon, his own interest in her was paramount. He worked the rest of the day around the house and helped his father with the ferry. His parents were not surprised when he announced that he would be having dinner with Elizabeth at the tavern that evening. He was excited about spending time with Elizabeth, but he was also anxious about her reaction to his suspicions concerning Simon. After cleaning himself up and putting on some fresh clothes, he rode into town.

CHAPTER 17

Elizabeth walked out the front door of the boarding house at the same time Robert tied his horse to the hitching post. She was excited about having dinner together and had been watching out the door for him.

"I was just about to come out and sit in a rocking chair," she said shyly.

"We can sit awhile if you want," Robert responded.

"Oh no, I'm looking forward to my first time to have dinner at the tavern," Elizabeth announced.

"You ready?" Robert asked.

"Ready," Elizabeth responded with a smile and a nod.

"I have only eaten there a few times myself. There aren't many options here in town. I hope you're not disappointed. It would be nice to have a decent restaurant in town like some of those I have visited in McCormick or Lincolnton."

Elizabeth said, "I'm sure it will be fine. It's hard to believe that anyone in town could cook as well as Mrs. Norman. She is such a wonderful baker. Have you ever tasted her caramel cake? It is the best ever."

"I can't say as I have."

"She also bakes an amazing coconut cake. Did you know that she used to bake and sell wedding cakes to couples getting married?"

"I don't think I knew that. As you know, we're new-comers to the town."

"We can talk with her about possibly having a meal together at the boarding house sometime. She could set us up in the formal dining room."

"I like the sound of that."

Elizabeth continued, "Someone told me that Petersburg was a thriving farm town twenty years ago. Is that true?"

"I was too young to remember, but my parents told us stories about times when they came from Parksville to shop and dine out. Once, they spent the night at a boarding house in town. Not the one where you live now, but another one that's been abandoned for years. They met friends there and danced to a string quartet late into the night."

"Sounds wonderful," Elizabeth proclaimed. "I like dancing."

Robert went on avoiding Elizabeth's comment about dancing. As best he could remember, he had never danced before, and he had no intentions of doing so anytime soon. "To hear them talk, it's easy to understand how this was the place to be. The kind of town where people came to enjoy themselves. I heard that some of the local wealthy families hosted galas and balls as well as traveling artists and musicians. Nothing within fifty miles of here compared. Now it's mostly just a lot of older buildings and houses that have been abandoned. Sometimes when it's late at night and quiet, I can almost imagine hearing the lively music from town carried by the wind."

Robert pointed ahead to a large vacant building with a collapsed front porch, "That used to be a tobacco warehouse. There's only one still standing, and if cotton has its way, it will soon look just as bad as this one."

"Your father said that you were tobacco farmers."

"Yes, but that was before the fire," Robert added.

"The fire," Elizabeth looked surprised.

"We lost our home as a result of our tobacco barn burning."

During the rest of the stroll, Robert told Elizabeth how they had lost the farm and moved from Parksville.

He emphasized his desire to get back into farming, and that he was planning to purchase a farm and grow cotton.

After they entered the tavern, Robert selected a table and offered a chair to Elizabeth. Looking around, he noticed that there were only four other people in the tavern. Two men were playing cards at a table on the opposite side of the room, and another man was standing at the bar talking to the bartender. The bartender walked over. Robert said, "We would like to order something to eat."

"I have a limited menu tonight. It's either stew with potatoes, or potatoes with stew. What'll it be?" The bartender stared at them with an expressionless face that was hard to read.

Robert looked at the man and then back at Elizabeth, "I don't know. Elizabeth, what would you like?"

Elizabeth rolled her eyes and put her hand under her chin, "Let's see. I think I will have the stew with potatoes."

"That sounds good, but the potatoes with stew sounds delicious. I'll have the potatoes with stew," Robert replied.

"Good choice," the bartender's voice growled.

"Do you drink sweet tea?" Robert asked looking at Elizabeth.

"Yes, that sounds fine."

"We would also like two sweet teas please."

Once the man walked away, Robert and Elizabeth looked at one another and broke out in laughter.

"Nothing like southern hospitality," Elizabeth laughed.

"We were lucky. Friends told me that he gets really grumpy late in the day."

The bartender returned shortly after with two glasses of tea. "Your food will be right out," he said turning towards the bar again.

"May I ask a question?" Robert's expression and tone changed while making eye contact with Elizabeth.

"Of course," Elizabeth answered after sipping her tea.

"I know you have been seeing Simon Hale. How well do you know him?"

Elizabeth looked at him with one raised eyebrow, "That's an interesting question. Why do you ask?"

Robert continued, "Look, please don't be upset with me, it's just that I…," Robert's words trailed off. He paused. "Well, I don't know how to say this except to just go ahead and say it out loud. I don't trust him."

Elizabeth sat up straight, raised both eyebrows, and gently shook her head from side to side, "Well Robert, I thought that I was beginning to get to know you, but I must admit I am surprised to hear you say that. Are you jealous?"

"Please don't be angry. I am only trying to help you."

"Help me! How does that help me? I appreciate your concern, but I am fully capable of helping myself."

Robert looked around the room trying to find the right words to say. He had to admit to himself that there was something about her wit and candor that was attractive. He was treading on thin ice and knew it. He thought for a moment and opened his mouth just as he looked up and saw the bartender returning to the table with two steaming bowls.

When the bartender turned to walk away, Robert leaned towards Elizabeth and spoke so as not to be heard by others, "I'm not the only one who feels this way about Simon. My good friend Christopher Murphy works here at night. He feels the same way as I do."

"You are entitled to your feelings. But I am telling you that I think you and Christopher are wrong. Simon has been nothing but a gentleman."

Robert dipped his spoon in the stew, blew away the steam, and tasted it. "How do you like the stew?"

"It tastes really good. I'm pleasantly surprised."

"I agree," he said. "You said that your father is a preacher, right?"

"Yes."

Robert asked with a smile, "Did you ever imagine that you would be eating in a saloon?"

"I prefer to think of it as a tavern. It just sounds more appropriate. Anyway, I am not bothered in the least by being here."

"What do you think your students would say if they saw you here?" Robert asked.

"I think they would say that I chose to have a meal in the tavern. In my estimation, that should be the end of it."

"That's a great way to look at it," Robert continued enjoying another spoonful from the steaming bowl. "My parents would not agree with me drinking alcohol. I think that's why they haven't had a meal in the tavern since we moved to Petersburg."

Elizabeth paused thinking about Robert's comment, "It could be more than that. Maybe they just don't want to spend the money."

"Maybe so," Robert responded.

The bartender returned to ask if they would like more stew or tea. Robert looked at Elizabeth, then at the bartender, and declined. While the bartender stood by the table Robert asked, "Do you know Simon Hale?"

"Why yes, he is one of our best customers."

Robert was a bit stunned by the positive response. He hoped that his question would have resulted in a negative reaction. Elizabeth glared at Robert with dagger-like eyes.

This was not going well. Robert's strategy to discredit Simon was failing miserably.

"Will that do it for you two?" the bartender asked.

"Yes, it will. I think I've had quite enough," Elizabeth answered abruptly putting her napkin on the table. The bartender gave a quizzical glance at Robert then returned to the bar area.

Elizabeth raised her chin, looked Robert in the eye, and said, "Robert, I like you a lot, but I see no reason for you to be critical of my friends. For the most part, this has been a pleasant experience, but you have consistently tried to discredit Simon, and I can't understand why you are doing that. Based on what I've heard from you, I know Simon better than you do."

Robert did not have an answer. Elizabeth was clearly upset, and Robert was desperate to come up with an answer to his dilemma. Somehow, he had to convince Elizabeth that Simon had a dark heart despite his outward appearance.

Robert walked to the bar and paid the tab for dinner. He walked back to where Elizabeth was still seated and pulled her chair back for her. Standing she led the way to the door. Elizabeth reluctantly agreed to take a stroll through town. They had not gone far when Robert looked towards Simon's cotton office and warehouse and saw one of his wagons loaded with cotton bales. The wagon was parked in the alley. It was ready to be used to transport cotton to the mill early the next morning. The evening moon lit the street and buildings which were mostly abandoned or vacant at that hour. Robert recalled his conversation with Christopher who accused Simon of transporting and selling moonshine from across the river into Georgia. Without saying anything, Robert moved away from Elizabeth while glancing over both shoulders.

"What are you doing?" Elizabeth questioned.

"This will only take a minute," Robert responded leaving Elizabeth standing in the middle of the street.

Robert moved slowly around all four sides of the wagon, momentarily stopping to reach his hand into the empty spaces between cotton bales. He hoped that he might discover containers used for the transportation of moonshine hidden among the bales.

"Robert, I'm ready to go home," Elizabeth demanded in a sharp voice.

Ignoring her plea, Robert continued his inspection until it became obvious that there were no hidden containers. He slowly walked back over to Elizabeth and explained the reason for his actions.

Elizabeth's body became tense and rigid as her gaze

turned away from Robert in the direction of the boarding house. "Take me home now, or I will walk by myself. I am convinced that you are jealous of Simon and his success as a business owner."

"But Elizabeth," he paused. "I don't want to see you get hurt."

"Hurt!" she replied loudly. "What reason would Simon have to hurt me? So far he's made me laugh and enjoy myself for the first time in months."

"I know what hurt feels like," Robert said.

Elizabeth let out a deep breath, turned without saying a word, and began walking towards the boarding house.

"Wait," Robert called out walking quickly to catch up with her.

After walking several city blocks without a word, Elizabeth broke her silence and asked, "Is there a message you would like me to deliver to Simon tomorrow?"

Robert stopped in his tracks, "What! Why are you seeing Simon tomorrow?"

She continued walking, "He has invited me to view a local farm he hopes to purchase that will be auctioned on Monday."

Robert was stunned. He also heard that the bank had foreclosed on another farm; however, he was not aware that the auction would be on Monday. The bank manager told him that the farm would not be ready to sell for at least another month. He was beginning to feel like the process to auction the farms was rigged, and that the bank was giving preference to someone.

"Well, do you?"

"Do I what?" Robert was so lost in thought that he did not hear her question.

"Do you have a message for Simon?"

"No," he said abruptly looking away.

They walked the rest of the way back to the boarding house without saying a word. After passing through the gate, Elizabeth thanked Robert for buying her dinner, then turned towards the porch. Robert watched in silence as she opened the front door, entered, and closed it behind her without a second glance. Robert didn't want to admit it, but it seemed that their relationship had turned as cold as the late evening October breeze. He had hoped for a better outcome. Even though Elizabeth thought Simon trustworthy, he wasn't convinced that Simon could be trusted. Robert thought about going to the site of the auction the next day.

CHAPTER 18

Elizabeth ate breakfast alone on Sunday morning. Kate had prepared scrambled eggs, sausage, and toast for her boarders before leaving to go to church to teach Sunday school. The only active church in town was a small Methodist congregation. Following breakfast, Elizabeth walked to church and entered just as the service was about to begin. Kate Norman saw Elizabeth enter and motioned for her to come join her on the pew.

"I am so glad that you decided to join me," Kate whispered. "Please sit."

"This is where I needed to be. I have missed being in worship. I'm looking forward to hearing your minister."

After singing the closing hymn, they walked out together and thanked the minister for the service. Elizabeth agreed to return next Sunday. Kate asked Elizabeth about her evening with Robert and her plans for that afternoon.

"It's all very confusing. I like Robert, but he did everything possible last night to discredit Simon Hale."

"How did that make you feel?"

"I was angry at first, and I'm still upset by it all."

Kate said, "I have seen Simon a few times at the boarding house, but that was long before you came to town. He seems to be a decent person. Tell me about school."

"School is going great. I am enjoying the students and slowly getting to know their families."

"That's good news. By the way, I meant to ask what your father had to say in his letter?"

Elizabeth's tried to hide her sadness. "He is doing well but could not say when he would be able to visit. I was hoping that he could get away from Milledgeville for a few days."

"I know that is disappointing, but you have much to be thankful for. Many families have been torn apart by poor decisions or circumstances they never intended."

"I know you're right. I just miss them so much. Sometimes it's all I can think about."

"That's normal, Elizabeth. Your mother just passed away. That is something that will always be with you, but it does not have to define you. You know what they say, keep your chin up." Kate sighed. She stopped and looked at Elizabeth, "I'm here for you anytime you feel sad, or alone. All you have to do is walk downstairs."

Having returned to the boarding house Kate said, "I'll see you in a little while. I need to get lunch ready."

"Let me help," Elizabeth offered.

"Sure, come on. We can do this together."

They prepared lunch which consisted of food left over from Saturday. After a quick meal, Elizabeth thanked Kate for their discussion and for lunch, then she went to her room to change clothes and freshen up. On her way up the stairs, she remembered Ruth telling her about going away for the weekend on a visit to see a family member in Augusta.

It was a beautiful October afternoon without a cloud in the sky when Simon arrived in his horse-drawn carriage with a fold-down top. Hearing the sound, Elizabeth walked out onto the front porch and approached the fence gate. She waved to Simon as he got out of the carriage and met her at the gate.

"Are you ready to see my next cotton farm?" Simon asked after opening the gate and extending his hand to assist Elizabeth into the carriage. He walked around the front of the carriage and joined her on the seat. They continued their discussion during the ride to the farm.

"Do you plan to purchase this farm?" Elizabeth asked.

"That's my plan but only if the price is right. It will depend on whether anyone bids against me. I doubt that will happen since most people around here are selling, not buying. Now, I want to hear more about your dinner date last night."

"How did you know I was on a dinner date?"

"One of my employees was at the tavern and saw you with your friend. He said that you two seemed to be having an argument."

Elizabeth was embarrassed that anyone might have overheard her conversation with Robert at the tavern. She wondered how much, if anything, Simon knew about what Robert had done on their walk following dinner. It would have been humiliating for her if someone had seen Robert digging around in the load of cotton. She couldn't help but wonder if Simon already knew.

Simon continued, "Look, I know more about Robert than he thinks. A failed tobacco farm, his previous relationship issues with a young woman in town, and his attempts to talk the bank into loaning him money to purchase a farm. What else would you like to know?"

"What do you mean by his relationship issues?"

"Elizabeth, are you the only person in town who doesn't know that Anna Smith became pregnant by Robert?"

Elizabeth was shaken by the announcement. She sat up straight in the carriage seat trying to disguise her shock. "I'm not sure what to say right now."

"I didn't want to be the one to tell you, but I thought you should know," Simon continued.

"How do you know if that is even true?" Elizabeth asked.

"Well, let's just say it came from a reliable source."

Elizabeth stared blankly ahead; eyes fixed on the road. The only sound for a moment was the horses' hooves hitting the hard-packed dirt road.

She was awakened from her trance by Simon's voice, "You okay?"

"Oh, yes! I'm just trying to process what you told me. Having met Robert, it just seems so unlike him. You could have blown me over with a feather just now."

"I am sorry, but I felt that it was my duty to tell you since you have chosen to spend time with him."

It was true that she wanted to spend more time getting to know Robert, but this was all so confusing. She began to wonder if seeing him was a mistake.

They arrived at the site of the foreclosure. Elizabeth saw an unfamiliar man riding towards them on a horse. Simon again assisted Elizabeth while she stepped out of the carriage. Simon looked around and swept his hand in front of him. "I think this will work out well. The old farmhouse is run down, but the farm will be perfect. I can almost see the field white with cotton and my bank account green with cash."

The man on horseback approached the carriage. "Hello, Simon! Are you also interested in buying this farm?" the man asked.

"Fred, I didn't think I would see you here today. The answer to your question is yes; I intend to purchase the farm," Simon replied with confidence.

"I see!" The man looked at Elizabeth. "Mornin', miss! My name is Fred Taylor."

That name sounded familiar to Elizabeth, but she couldn't place where she had heard it before. "Good day Mr. Taylor, I am Elizabeth Bright."

"Aren't you the new schoolteacher?"

"Yes, I am."

"Then you know Robert Chambers. Robert works for me, and he was telling me about his plans to have dinner with you."

"As a matter of fact, we had dinner together last night."

"How long has Robert worked for you?" Simon interrupted.

"It's been a few months now. Why do you ask?"

"I would keep my eye on him if I were you," Simon announced.

"What do you mean?"

"It might not look good for such an upstanding businessman as yourself to employee someone with his reputation, but it's really none of my business whom you hire."

"I'm a rather good judge of character. I admit that he is quiet, but he seems to do well for himself."

Simon continued, "If you say so. Anyway, I hear he's looking to buy a farm of his own, so I doubt he will work for you much longer. You might get lucky if the bank agrees to loan him the money."

Fred looked at Elizabeth, "It was nice to meet you, Miss Bright. Please let me know if there is anything I can do for you. It's not every day we have such a beautiful young lady move to town."

"Thank you, Mr. Taylor," she responded. "That is very kind of you."

"I will let Robert know that I met you."

"Please do," Elizabeth said. "He told me that he might come by to look at the property himself."

"I hope that he does if he is interested in buying a farm."

Mr. Taylor pulled on the front of his cap, nodded

toward Simon, and rode away. Elizabeth watched and reflected on what she heard. Simon continued to point describing his plans for the property.

"So, what do you think?" Simon asked.

Elizabeth turned towards him lost in her thoughts, "What? Oh, yes," she said. "I don't know much about farming, but this seems to be a nice place." She was growing weary of Simon and Robert going after one another like two roosters in a barnyard. She enjoyed being with Simon, but she was concerned about his character after hearing him make accusations about Robert. She didn't know if what she heard was rumor or fact. She could almost hear the voice of her father warning her about the potential harm that could come from spreading rumors. Why did they seem to dislike one another? Was it jealousy or something more sinister?

Chapter 19

Frank Parks was working late in his store Sunday night putting away a shipment of supplies in preparation for the coming week. Thanksgiving was approaching, and the citizens of Parksville depended on goods from Frank's store to get them through the holidays.

A single lantern provided just enough light at the back of the store for him to get his work done. He was sweeping the floor when a sound coming from the front of the store startled him. He walked down the center aisle in the dim light toward the sound and reached for an unlit lantern that he kept in the middle of the store.

James Ridley stepped from behind a counter and struck Frank on the back of the head with an axe handle. Frank immediately crumpled to the floor and lay motionless. James looked around and moved quickly to the back of the store. Mr. Parks kept detailed records of all the farmers in the area. It was his way of ensuring the creditworthiness of his customers. Each farmer, who used his credit for goods, filled out a card designating the name, address, acreage, and owner of the farm. Simon Hale intended to use this information to identify all the local tobacco farmers in the region that were at a credit risk. The information would tell him which farmers were behind on their payments to the store. This would allow him to get ahead of the bank and approach farmers who were near foreclosure on their farms. He intended to make desperately low offers to purchase their farms before they lost everything.

The lantern was still burning when James walked past the interior window and counter that served as the Parksville post office. Seeing his face pictured on a wanted poster, he pulled the poster down and stuffed it into his overall pocket. "Won't be needing this one," he sneered through gritted teeth. James had seen the poster earlier during the week when Simon sent him to check out the layout of the store. He moved quickly in case Frank regained consciousness. Opening an upright filing cabinet, he found the card file that contained the customer account records. James began leafing through the cards and pulled out several which he stuffed into the same pocket where he had put the wanted poster. He failed to realize that when he pushed the last few cards into his overalls, the crumpled wanted poster fell to the floor. Once he had what he came for, he walked past the motionless body of Frank Parks and out into the cold darkness.

—

NEWS OF THE DEATH of Frank Parks spread quickly in the community the next morning. Sheriff Davidson informed William Chambers while crossing the river just after daybreak while on his way from Parksville to Petersburg.

"I can't believe it," William said. "Frank and I have been friends for years. I can't tell you the number of times he gave us food on credit until our crops came in. This is such a tragedy for our community. Robert will take this hard. Frank helped him get a job. Would you mind telling Robert for me?"

"Where can I find Robert?" Joseph asked.

"He is already at the Taylor farm."

"Thank you, Mr. Chambers," Joseph replied just before he rode away.

Robert was shocked to hear about the loss of his good friend Frank Parks.

Joseph said, "I'm here to speak with the Petersburg

sheriff about the incident. I will be headed back to Mr. Park's store soon."

"I want to go with you. Frank was my friend."

"I don't see any harm in that. Come on."

After they visited the local sheriff, the two men mounted up and rode back to the ferry.

Robert told his father, "I will be back soon. I want to visit the scene with Joseph."

"Okay, Son," William answered.

Once inside the store, Robert walked deliberately along the walls and between each aisle of merchandise. The sheriff found a partly opened filing cabinet drawer containing a small metal card file that had been turned over spilling cards into the back of the drawer.

"Robert, come over here and look at this," Joseph called out.

Robert looked at the open file box, "Joseph, Frank would not have left these confidential account cards out for someone to find. He was too neat and organized for that. Someone else did this."

Robert looked down and picked up a crumpled piece of paper on the floor. After unfolding the paper, he showed it to Joseph. They looked at the scarred face of James Ridley. Robert recalled his conversation with Frank about a concern that James might be back in the area.

Joseph handed the poster back to Robert, "I want you to take this poster back to Petersburg and show it to the sheriff. I want to see if he can supply any more information on this Ridley character."

Robert agreed and rode away, leaving Joseph at the scene. Robert stopped long enough at the ferry to show the poster to his father.

William said, "I think I have seen this man. Maybe once. Come to think about it, a man with similar features crossed the ferry with Simon not long ago."

"Where were they going?" Robert asked.

"I don't know. They stayed to themselves and didn't speak to anyone."

Robert told his father goodbye and rode on to town. Not far from the Petersburg sheriff's office, he saw Elizabeth crossing the street near the tavern.

"Good morning," Robert said.

"Hello Robert," Elizabeth looked at Robert shielding her eyes from the sun.

"Why aren't you at school?"

"This is a planning day for the teachers. Didn't Susie tell you?"

"I got an early start this morning, and she was still asleep when I left home," Robert said getting down from the horse.

"Where are you going in such a hurry?" Elizabeth asked.

"My friend Frank Parks has been murdered. The sheriff in Parksville asked me to show this wanted poster to the sheriff here in Petersburg. We found it at the scene."

Robert pulled the poster out of his pocket and handed it to Elizabeth.

"I am so sorry to hear about your friend." Elizabeth took the poster, gasped, and raised her hand to her mouth.

"What is it?" Robert asked.

"Do you remember me telling you about the convict who threatened my father and me the night my mother died? I think this is the same man."

"Would you come with me and tell that to the sheriff?" Robert asked.

"I guess that I could if you think it would help, but after we leave his office, I have something to ask you."

"Sure. Come on. We can walk from here."

Robert and Elizabeth took the poster to Sheriff Edward Scott, and Elizabeth explained why she believed that she had seen James before. The sheriff was unable to make any immediate connections but told them that he would begin an investigation. Robert also told the sheriff about a possible connection with Simon based on the information his father reported about seeing them together. At the sound of Simon's name, Elizabeth turned abruptly towards Robert with a look of concern on her face. She was clearly not happy with Robert for bringing up Simon's name, especially in front of the sheriff.

The sheriff raised an eyebrow, paused as if contemplating his response, and put the poster face down on his desk.

"Now that is interesting. Thanks for the information. I will let you know what turns up."

They walked out of the office and stepped into the morning sun that still hung low enough on the horizon that it cast long shadows from the trees and buildings.

"I got the feeling that the sheriff didn't really care," Robert said to Elizabeth.

With a wrinkled brow, Elizabeth turned to Robert, "I need you to be honest with me about something."

"That doesn't sound good."

"It's about Anna."

"What! How do you know Anna?"

"I was with Simon …."

Before she could get the rest of the sentence out, Robert cut her off. "Simon! I should have known. What lies is he spreading now?"

"As I was saying before you rudely interrupted. Simon and I were together yesterday. He told me that you were the father of Anna Smith's child."

Robert's face turned red, and his lips flattened out. He

looked up as if waiting for a sign from above. He could feel his pulse rising and the veins in his neck throbbing. His response was loud and direct. "This is ridiculous, and it must stop. How many times do I have to say this? I am not the father of any child, especially one with Anna."

Elizabeth stood and faced him. Speechless.

"I'm so sorry Elizabeth. I didn't mean to take it out on you. Please forgive me." Robert lowered his voice and explained that it was Frank Parks who had told him about seeing Anna and Thomas Wright together during the time that he and Anna were still dating.

"I broke up with Anna just after hearing that she was also seeing Thomas. Look Elizabeth! It is important that you believe me."

"I have no reason not to believe you, Robert. I just needed to hear it from you."

"Elizabeth, I want more than anything to spend more time with you. You have been a breath of fresh air. But this whole situation with Anna is making me look bad in the community, and now you seem to believe it as well."

Robert glanced up just as Thomas Wright walked out the front door of his father's bank.

"Follow me," Robert commanded walking at a fast pace in the direction of the bank. Robert was a compassionate and peaceful person, but at that moment, he decided that enough was enough and he was going to take matters into his own hands.

"Thomas!" Robert shouted closing the distance between them.

"Robert?" Thomas asked startled.

"We need to talk," Robert barked.

When Thomas turned in Robert's direction, the wind blew open his full-length overcoat, revealing the handle of a holstered pistol. Elizabeth caught up to where the two men were standing face-to-face in the middle of the street.

"Aren't you Elizabeth Bright?" Thomas asked looking at her.

"Yes, I am! Do I know you?"

"I guess not. I have a friend who was telling me about Robert and his new girlfriend."

Robert interrupted loudly, "I know about you and Anna."

"Know what?" Thomas blurted.

Robert glared at Thomas and felt his pulse pounding. "I know that Anna lost a baby that she was carrying. I know that I was not the father. I know that you were going out with Anna before we broke up. In fact, we broke up when I found out about the two of you." Robert's intensity grew with each accusation resulting in a standoff.

"Are you accusing me of getting Anna pregnant?"

"Damn right, I am!" Robert stepped in closer.

Thomas laughed out loud, "You're insane. Did it ever occur to you that Anna was going out with several men as she has done for years now? Why don't you ask Simon Hale about that?"

Elizabeth looked up immediately at Thomas and asked, "What does Simon have to do with this?"

"You two would make a good vaudeville act. Wake up and smell the coffee children," Thomas scoffed.

"Are you saying that Simon Hale has had an affair with Anna?" Robert asked.

"I'm saying that you need to ask him about that," Thomas answered with a chuckle. "I would love to continue our little chat, but I have business to take care of." Thomas turned and walked away.

"Now do you believe what I have been telling you about Simon?" Robert asked Elizabeth.

"I don't know what to believe anymore," Elizabeth spoke sounding frustrated. "I have to go."

"Where are you going?" Robert asked.

"I have papers to grade. I will most likely be at school until it's time for me to go home for dinner."

Elizabeth turned and began walking away.

"Is it okay if I call on you again for dinner?"

Elizabeth stopped briefly to turn and face him, "I'm not going to answer that right now."

Reluctantly, Robert walked back to the sheriff's office to retrieve his horse while Elizabeth continued in the direction of the school.

CHAPTER 20

Just before dark that evening, Robert decided to walk from home to the tavern. Even though he knew it would take a long time, he needed to process today's events. He intended to have dinner with Christopher. The sun dropped below the horizon and the night sky began to brighten. The blood-red harvest moon illuminated the surrounding area casting shadows from the town's buildings which appeared framed in gray and black.

He replayed the earlier events of the day. There was something about being out in nature that calmed his spirit, even when life around him was spinning like a twister. His anger had been red-hot listening to the way Thomas described Anna. Not that he cared, he had already suffered enough because of Anna, but it was still hard to hear, especially from someone with the arrogance of Thomas Wright. If his conversation with Thomas had been compared to a schoolyard fight, then Robert knew that he had been beaten when he was unable to answer Thomas. Robert couldn't help but wonder if his relationship with Elizabeth was over. She seemed terribly upset at their last parting. And then there was Simon. There was always Simon, whose name kept popping up in all kinds of conversations.

Entering town, he walked past the front of Simon's cotton warehouse and office. He noticed that the front office door was partly open. There was no light coming from inside and the building appeared deserted.

He paused and looked up and down the street. Seeing no one, he walked closer to investigate. "I really should just let this go," he thought to himself. "This is none of my business." Against his better judgment, he decided to walk over. Maybe Simon was in the warehouse and would round the corner at any minute.

He called Simon's name out loud while pushing the door open further. Hearing no response, he began to pull the door shut, when something on a small table near the door caught his attention. Incandescent moonlight shown through a nearby window illuminating a small ladies' brooch on the table. It looked familiar to him, so he pushed the door open, walked over, and picked it up. In the dim light, he could see that the pin on the back of the brooch was bent. This appeared to be the same brooch that he had given Anna early in their relationship. Could Thomas have been right about Simon and Anna? How did a brooch that he gave Anna end up in Simon's office? Could this be proof that she was also seeing Simon? There was also the possibility that the bent pin might have allowed the brooch to fall from Anna's clothing and that Simon had found it and was keeping it for her.

An even darker thought entered his mind. What if Anna had been with Simon in his home, and at some point, she had removed her clothing when the brooch caught something and pulled off? Transfixed by his thoughts, he did not hear Christopher walk in behind him.

"Robert!" Christopher called. "What are you doing in here?"

Quickly turning, Robert stared into the face of his good friend who looked perplexed.

"I was just walking past when...," Robert's words were interrupted by Simon.

"What the hell?" Simon demanded. "Why are you in my office? What are you looking for?"

Christopher interjected, "Simon was at the tavern having a drink. I overheard him telling someone that he was not sure he had locked his office door, so I offered to quickly run down and check it for him."

"What do you have there?" Simon asked pointing to the brooch in Robert's hand.

Robert seemed shocked looking from Simon then to Christopher, "Like I was just telling Christopher, I decided to walk to town tonight and couldn't help but notice when I passed your office that the door was not fully closed."

Simon interrupted, "So you just decided at that moment to become a good Samaritan, even though we both know you hate my guts?"

"No…well, yes I…," Simon cut Robert off again in mid-sentence.

"I think the sheriff will be most interested in hearing about this break-in and attempted robbery. How many other businesses have you broken into lately?"

"I did not break in," Robert shouted. Veins bulged in his neck. "The door was already open."

Christopher was speechless.

"You believe me don't, you?" Robert pleaded with his friend, "I didn't break…"

"Put the brooch down and get out," Simon shouted. "I will take this up with the sheriff tomorrow morning."

"Where did you get this?" Robert asked accusingly.

"That's none of your business and there is no

need in trying to change the subject. Put it down," Simon demanded.

Robert knew it was pointless to plead his case. He had been caught red-handed in the wrong place at the wrong time. He gently placed the brooch back on the table.

Robert and Christopher walked out leaving Simon who quickly pulled the door shut and locked it.

"I don't know what just happened in there, but this is not going to look good." Christopher sounded annoyed.

"Christopher, I did not break in. I was just passing by and saw the open door."

"Then why didn't you just shut it and walk away?"

"I started to and then I saw the brooch. I thought that it could prove a connection between Simon and Anna."

"What connection?" Christopher asked.

Robert told Christopher about the discussion between him and Thomas earlier that day.

"And you say that Elizabeth heard all of this?" Christopher asked.

"Yes, she did. What am I gonna do?" Robert asked his friend.

"Well, you can start by telling the truth."

"Christopher!" Robert snapped. "When was the last time I lied to you?"

"All right, I get it, but I'm just saying that you were

not thinking clearly when you went into Simon's office without permission."

Robert took his hat and slapped it hard against his thigh, "You're right. I should have just walked away and left his office door open."

"Come on, I've got to get back to the tavern. We can talk about it there," Christopher barked.

The two men walked most of the way back to the tavern in silence while Simon went in the direction of his home. Nearing the entrance, Christopher stopped and turned to Robert. "I have a confession," he said.

"Okay," Robert replied.

"The real reason I went to help Simon in the first place was because he had just handed me the biggest tip I've ever seen. It was equal to a month's wage at the tavern. I was just trying to do him a favor in return. So when Simon walked in behind us I was embarrassed and angry."

"Christopher, please believe me, I did not intend to go into Simon's office tonight."

"Look, I'm trying to sort all this out. Even I admit that you have been acting a little strange lately. You seem obsessed with Simon. You talk about him constantly."

Robert knew Christopher was angry, but Robert was angry too for being falsely accused. "I better go home. Knowing Simon, I feel sure he will not be able to let this go." And with that, he turned and walked away. His buddy shook his head in disbelief.

On his walk home, Robert studied the stars. The moon's brightness hid many from sight, but he could still make out the North Star. It reminded him of late-night coon hunting when he had to depend on the North Star to get his bearings and find his way out of the woods. Most of the time, Robert enjoyed being outdoors; it made him happy, but tonight there weren't enough stars in the sky to chase away his sadness. He felt like a failure. The relationships with all of his friends seemed to be falling apart. Arguments made Robert uncomfortable, but he couldn't understand why. Friends had told him that he was quiet and that he would allow others to run over him. Robert knew that he did not like to disappoint others. Thinking back, he realized that his family was also quiet in some ways. They loved to sit around after dinner to share stories and laughter but seldom shared their feelings, hurts, or disappointments with one another. He had seen the opposite whenever he visited Anna's home. Her family was not shy about sharing. They would openly discuss some of the most intimate details of life that Robert would never have discussed with his family. Somehow, it made Robert uncomfortable to be in the room when such conversations broke out.

He remembered when he was in school, the classroom bully seemed to zero in on him. He never really understood why he had been designated as his punching bag. Robert often returned home from school with bruises. He felt like he was back on the school playground with yet another bully. Thomas and Simon were the bullies this time. He was losing control of his emotions and thoughts. He had embarrassed Christopher and confused or offended Elizabeth. To make matters worse, he knew Elizabeth would soon learn of his latest conflict with Simon.

It was late when he arrived home. He sat on the porch steps hoping the sounds of the night would calm him. He could hear the soft gurgling sounds of the river. The crickets' chirps rang in his ear with an unceasing pattern. There were sounds of the male frogs along the shoreline who sent out signals for potential mates. An owl's hoot echoed through the pines. Robert looked up at the night sky again. Stars faded in and out, their beauty vibrant against the blackness. It was then he realized that he felt calmer, and his thoughts turned to things for which he could be thankful: family, home, and a job just being a few. A smile broke across his face when he thought of Elizabeth. He breathed deeply and closed his eyes trying to imagine her sitting beside him. He could almost smell her perfume and sense the touch of her hand that even now caused his skin to tingle. Of all the things he had to be thankful for, he was most thankful for the day that he first saw Elizabeth down by the river. His heart ached knowing that his recent actions might cause her to reject him. However, Elizabeth had changed his resolve to stay away from romantic relationships. He surprised himself with how his feelings for Elizabeth had changed his resolve to stay away from romantic relationships. Elizabeth was unlike anyone he had ever met. She was worth the risk even if it meant being hurt again.

Rising from the steps, he instinctively glanced back in the direction of Petersburg. A sinking feeling gripped him. Would Simon go to the sheriff? How would Elizabeth interpret what had happened? He let out a deep sigh, removed his hat, and turned the doorknob.

"Robert," he was startled to hear his name whispered.

"Mother, why are you still awake?" Robert asked.

"I couldn't sleep, so I came in here to sit a while. I hadn't been here but a few minutes when I heard you walk on the porch steps. I decided to wait for you to come in before going back to bed."

The room was softly lit by the natural ambient light coming through the windows.

Robert spoke with a soft voice, "I apologize if I caused you to be unable to sleep."

"Son," Martha whispered, "To be quite honest, I have had many sleepless nights in the last few months because of my concern for you. Come and sit."

Robert took a deep breath and sat down in a chair beside his mother. He studied the floor considering what to say next.

"Tell me what it was like when you first knew you were in love with Dad," Robert said looking up at his mother.

She leaned back in her chair and looked up with a smile.

"Your father and I first met four years after the end of the war between the states. His mother did not allow him to join the Confederate army because he was only thirteen at the time. He told me of his friends who went off to war and never returned. I was at a church bazaar," Martha laughed softly. "My family went to church every time the doors opened, but your father's family were the type that only came once a year at Easter. I think he would tell you that they did not attend church regularly because, to them, Sunday had become just another workday."

"That sounds familiar," Robert interjected.

"Yes, it does. I first spoke to him at the end of an Easter service while families gathered outside to eat. The children went in search of hidden colored eggs. I was following my baby sister trying to help her find an egg when your father and I accidentally bumped into each other. We both saw the same egg hidden in deep grass behind a tree. Being the gentleman that he is, he pulled his younger brother back allowing my sister to pick up the egg and put it in her basket. It's hard to describe what happened next," Martha paused.

"Please continue," Robert said. "I want to hear everything."

"Alright," she replied.

"Your father's brother had gathered twice as many eggs as my sister. I will never forget how he looked at the basket, then at me as he called his brother to the side and whispered something in his ear. His little brother walked back over and began slowly moving some of the eggs from his basket to my sister's basket. I looked up at your father and asked him what he had said to his brother that would cause him to do that."

"What did he say?" Robert asked.

"First, he told me that he had asked his brother if he had ever seen such a beautiful girl, referring to me. Then he asked him if he would be willing to help him get to know me better by sharing some of his eggs with my sister." The memory brought a smile to Martha's face. "From that time on, your father joined me in church almost every Sunday after getting permission from his family of course. That went on for about two years before we announced to our families that we were going to get married in that same church where we first met."

"I don't think you have ever told me that story. How did you know that he was the one?"

"There were many signs that convinced me that I wanted to spend the rest of my life with him. He was always kind and easy to talk to. We came from similar backgrounds and had the same interests. But I think the one thing more than anything else that let me know he loved me was the effort he made to be with me. He literally moved heaven and earth so that he could spend time with me. His father would not let him get out of working on Sunday, but he did allow him to take a few hours in the middle of the day so that he could join me at church. We would spend an hour or so together after he walked me home. He intentionally placed my interest above his own. I think real love becomes evident when couples commit to work through difficult times. People in love will always experience difficulties and challenges. Love is the glue that allows two lives to stick together making it possible to work through any problems that are sure to come."

The two of them sat in silence. Robert began to reflect on his relationship with Anna. Even though he once thought that he was in love with Anna, looking back now, he realized that neither of them had been willing to put their interest above the interest of the other as his mother had described. He determined that if that was a foundation of being in love, then what he had experienced must have been something other than love.

Martha continued, "Son, I knew what kind of girl Anna was before you two began spending time together."

"What!" Robert turned suddenly and whispered, "Then why didn't you tell me?"

"If you remember, we tried to discourage you early on, but you were too infatuated at that point to hear us."

His mother was right, and Robert knew it. "I won't make that mistake again," he said.

"I'm sure you won't, but at the same time, don't let that stop you from trying to love again."

The two of them talked quietly for several minutes before slipping off to bed. Robert shared everything he knew about Anna and Thomas. He also shared his concerns about Ruth and the latest episode with Simon. Later, in his bed, he closed his eyes and thought of Elizabeth. Had he been putting her interest above his own? The thought troubled him. Was he simply infatuated with Elizabeth in the same way his mother had described his relationship with Anna, or could it be more? He hoped it could be more but how would he mend the damage he had done?

CHAPTER 21

The next morning, Simon looked out the window and saw the sheriff riding by on his way to the jail. Simon was near the door before the sheriff could get the key in the lock.

"Edward!" Simon called out still at some distance. Simon had known Edward Scott since he first moved to Petersburg.

"Simon! What do you want?"

"I have a little job for you."

"What is it now? Did the town drunk steal another jar of your moonshine?" Edward asked with a chuckle.

"Very funny! I just caught Robert Chambers trying to take something from my office."

"Simon, you know I have asked before that you stop bothering me with petty issues."

Simon continued recounting the story from last night. The sheriff did his best to patiently listen.

"I will speak with Robert. Is that good enough for now?"

Simon looked over the shoulder of the sheriff and noticed the wrinkled wanted poster of James Ridley that was pinned to the wall directly behind the sheriff's desk. "How did that get here?"

"I'm not prepared to discuss it now."

"Take that poster down!"

"That's not a good idea. What if the person that gave it to me came back and found it missing? How would I explain that?"

"I don't care how you explain it. Take it down or I will." When Edward did not react, Simon reached for the poster and snatched it off the wall.

Edward stood, faced Simon, and pointed towards the door, "Get out!"

Simon glared at the sheriff as he pushed the wanted poster into the pocket of his overcoat and walked out.

Even before going to the sheriff's office, Simon had already made plans to accomplish two things today. First, he would cross the river and pay a visit to James. Secondly, he would stop by the schoolhouse late that afternoon to speak with Elizabeth. He couldn't wait to tell her the latest news about Robert.

—

"How did your wanted poster find its way to the sheriff's office in Petersburg?" Simon barked at James.

James looked up from the table where he had just opened a can of beans. "It's only a poster. Why are you giving me such a hard time about it? I took it from the old man's store in Parksville. I guess it fell out of my pocket."

"You guess it fell out of your pocket. I told you to get in and out without touching anything except the credit files," Simon blurted. "You not only touched things, but you hit and killed the store owner."

"How was I supposed to know he was still working? The store was dark except for a small lantern in the very back. I didn't want to hurt him. He left me no choice. He was about to catch me red-handed in his store, so I knocked him out."

"Don't expect any more trips with me to the tavern or anywhere else near Petersburg," Simon scolded. "You will have to lay low for a while. I can't afford to make any more mistakes. Once I have all of the information I need, then I will pay you off with enough money to get you far away from here. If you're smart, you will take the money and never come back."

Wiping bean juice from his chin, James stood to face off with Simon, "Did you just threaten me?"

Simon stepped towards James while placing his hand on the top of his holstered revolver. James was a broad, burly man, but Simon towered above him. "That's not a threat, it's a promise!" Simon exited the dilapidated cabin forcefully slamming the door almost breaking it free from its rusty hinges. He mounted his horse and rode towards the ferry.

Robert's father was working the ferry that morning. Simon, along with several other customers, loaded to cross. He avoided William and had no plans to speak with him about the incident with Robert.

"Good morning Simon?"

"Same to you, Mr. Chambers."

"I meant to tell you that Ruth Garrett stopped by a few days ago asking about you. I think she spoke with Robert out in the yard."

"Ruth Garrett! I have no idea why she would be asking about me."

"She just asked if I'd seen you that morning. Maybe Robert could tell you more, but he's at work right now."

"Thanks for the information."

———

NEAR THE END OF the workday, Simon rode to the schoolhouse. He hoped that Ruth had already gone home for the day. He did not want an embarrassing moment should he find both women together. Elizabeth was sitting alone at her desk with papers spread out before her when Simon entered.

"Simon, hello! I didn't expect to see you here."

"How are you, Elizabeth? Do you have a moment?"

"Sure! What is it?"

"Robert is becoming quite the unsavory character."

Elizabeth interrupted Simon. She stood with a look of concern, "Please, not Robert again. Simon, I like you, but all this talk about Robert needs to stop."

Without hesitating Simon continued, "He broke into my office last night."

"What!" Elizabeth responded in disbelief and slowly sat back down.

"I caught him myself. His friend Christopher is a witness."

"Why would Robert break into your office?"

"I'm sure the sheriff will answer that soon enough."

"The sheriff," Elizabeth gasped.

"Well of course. After all, he committed a crime, didn't he?"

Elizabeth sat motionless staring at the papers in front of her. She could not process what she was hearing. She breathed in deeply letting it out slowly while looking out the window towards the playground. What next, she thought to herself. This was too much drama for her, especially since she was still suffering from the loss of her mother and the absence from her father. For the first time since moving to Petersburg, she began to think that she might be better off leaving town at the end of the school year. She could always move back in with her father and seek a job closer to home.

She finally spoke, changing the subject, "Thank you, Simon, but as you can see I am busy. By the way, did you purchase the farm you showed me?"

"Closed the deal yesterday," Simon answered. "Sorry if I ruined your day. Just thought you needed to know. I am counting on having dinner with you again. How about tonight?"

Elizabeth felt uncomfortable with Simon's persistence, especially when considering the concerns she had heard from Robert. She took a deep breath, "I appreciate the invitation, but, I think it would be best if we pause our relationship for a time."

"Have I said something wrong?" Simon asked.

"No. I just need time to think. Anyway, my schoolwork is just consuming all of my spare time at the moment."

Simon continued, "So I guess that means you won't be spending more time with Robert either?"

"I guess not," she said frowning.

Simon turned and walked out slamming the door behind him, startling Elizabeth.

She sighed deeply. Staring blindly at the back of the door, she felt lightheaded from Simon's latest revelation. Life was so much simpler back at home, she thought. Milledgeville was growing, which stood in sharp contrast to Petersburg. There would be more job opportunities hopefully in teaching and even more importantly, young men who wouldn't complicate her life. She longed for a stable relationship and a dependable man she could trust. She also missed hearing her father preach on Sundays. She knew she was prejudiced, but she had never heard anyone interpret scripture or give an inspiring message like her father.

Soon the dizziness began to fade away. An outing might do her good. A visit to the train depot in Vienna would give her an opportunity to inquire about the price of a train ticket to Milledgeville.

CHAPTER 22

Early Saturday morning, Robert hitched one of their horses to the wagon and saddled the other one for himself. William, Martha, and Susie got in the wagon ready to depart on a trip that had been planned a few weeks earlier. They were going to attend a fall festival in Lincolnton about an hour away. Posters had been placed at several locations in Petersburg announcing the dates of the festival. The owner of the ferry had found an assistant to help William on the weekends allowing them to leave town for a short time. Everyone was excited about getting away for the day.

In Lincolnton, local vendors set up tents and canopies around the two-story courthouse built on the public square. Smoke rose from small portable campfires used to provide hot food. Members of a local Methodist church sold drinks, cakes, pies, and more sweets than imaginable. Men sat in circles playing guitars and banjos. Many people stopped and sang along whenever they played a crowd favorite like *Virginia Belle* by Stephen Foster or hymns like *I'll Fly Away*. Susie and Martha giggled and dipped their faces into a large container filled with water and floating apples. Robert and William stopped to test their strength at a high striker. It proved too much for William, but Robert was able to connect every time. The sound of the ringing bell could be heard by everyone near the square.

When it was time for lunch, the family walked a short distance to sit at one of the tables set up near the food vendors. Martha packed a lunch for them to enjoy knowing it would save some money that could be used at the festival for fun or gifts.

"How about a ham sandwich?" Martha asked looking at each family member.

Susie quickly raised her hand, "Me please."

"I also have apples and carrots."

"That sounds great, Honey," William said taking a sandwich, an apple, and a cup of water poured from a small canteen Martha had packed. "You know, I think it has been over ten years since I was in Lincolnton. It looks a lot like I remember. Susie, what's been your favorite thing so far?"

"I liked the petting zoo," she said enthusiastically.

Martha added, "That was the closest I've ever been to a buffalo."

"We should come back and spend a night in the old Gibson Hotel over there," William pointed at a large two-story building nearby. The inn was painted white with many shutterless windows. Small porches adorned all sides. "I hear tell that the ghosts of Revolutionary War soldiers still roam the halls at night."

"William please, you're going to scare Susie," Martha said. William laughed and winked at Susie.

"Staying at the inn sounds like a wonderful idea," Martha continued. "What do you think Robert?"

"I would like that very much. I like it here. I say let's move here and start over."

"Well now, that's something to think about," William answered smiling. "What is it about Lincolnton that would make you want to live here?"

"It's not Petersburg. I bet I could buy a farm here."

"I understand, Son. Don't dwell on the past. We have much to be thankful for today. We have jobs and a roof over our heads, and new friends whose company we enjoy."

Robert looked around seeing people enjoying themselves

making music and singing, some were dancing, and he felt a sense of community. "Petersburg isn't prospering like this, and I'm not ready to make it my permanent home. There is so little opportunity there."

"You're right," William said. "I remember my father telling me about the time he first visited Lincolnton. That was just after his family moved to Parksville from Northumberland County, North Carolina."

"Go on," Martha prodded.

"It was before the war. He and his older brother rode together in the family wagon from Parksville. They crossed the river on a ferry that operated downstream from Petersburg. They came looking for jobs at the sewing plant in town. Farming was difficult. So after a few bad years, I guess the boys were looking for something better. They must have never found it because both of them returned to Parksville. Not long after that, they joined the Confederate army. My uncle was killed during the war."

Robert found his father's tales of the past entertaining; however, he was distracted with thoughts of Elizabeth. He was serious about moving to Lincolnton. At the same time, he was concerned about what that might mean to his relationship with Elizabeth. Robert was falling in love with Elizabeth but was unsure if she felt the same way about him.

On the ride home he summoned the courage to talk with his family about his feelings for Elizabeth.

"You're in love with Miss Bright?" Susie asked. She stood up and began jumping up and down in the back of the wagon.

Martha smiled broadly, "Now Susie, don't get too excited yet. Robert still has to have a long conversation about this with Miss Bright."

"I can't wait to tell Grace," Susie continued.

"Susie, no you can't do that," Robert frowned with concern.

"Your brother is right," Martha continued. "This is a personal matter between the two of them. It just wouldn't be right for Miss Bright to hear any of this from anyone else but Robert."

"But Grace loves Miss Bright too. She won't tell nobody," Susie said clapping her hands.

"Listen to your mother Susie," William said. "Your brother is having a private conversation with us. We are not going to repeat this to anyone. Okay?"

Susie stopped clapping, looked at her father, and softly agreed, "Okay."

William continued looking at Robert, "We are proud of you, Son. Who knows if this will ever become more serious, but speaking for your mother and me, we could not be happier for you. Elizabeth is a beautiful young lady in every way. We think very highly of her."

"I'm glad you're pleased. I still have my work cut out since she has also been spending time with Simon."

"I heard about Simon courting her," William said. "Simon seems nice enough I guess, but those two seem to be about as different as salt and pepper."

Robert laughed, "I agree. I just have to convince her of that."

"You don't have to convince her of anything, Son," Martha said smiling at Robert. "Remember what I told you about how I knew when your father fell in love with me?"

"You mean about him spending time with you?"

"I told you that he would move heaven and earth to be with me making me the object of his undivided attention."

"If it's okay with you both, and if it's not too late, I would like to stop in town and visit Elizabeth on our way home," Robert said.

William answered after receiving a nod of approval from Martha, "That would be fine with us. I can put away the horse and wagon when we get back."

———

That same morning, Elizabeth had made her way to Vienna in a hired carriage. She did not know the man who helped her at the ferry and wondered where the Chambers family had gone. After arriving at the train depot, she saw a long line of passengers waiting at the ticket window. She got in line behind a family who was talking about some town in Virginia they were going to visit, but the town was not familiar to Elizabeth. Taking a pleasure trip was a luxury for most; however, the depot seemed to be filled with passengers going to distant places. All around her, she could hear excited conversations and laughter. Surveying the depot, she couldn't help but notice two men standing alone at the very end of the walkway. She immediately recognized Simon, but it was the other man that caught her attention. He looked familiar to her, but she could not remember right away where she had seen him. Just then the man turned in her direction, and she immediately recognized him. It was James Ridley. The same escaped convict who had threatened her and her father at the hospital in Milledgeville. The very sight of him made her shiver. She tilted her head down and away from the two men allowing the brim of her hat to cover her face.

All the conversations with Robert about Simon came flooding back. Why would Simon be collaborating with a known criminal and escapee? Could she have been wrong about Simon? It was obvious that either Robert or Simon had been lying to her.

"Mam!" the sound seemed distant. "Mam!" The ticket master called loudly startling Elizabeth from her thoughts. "Can I help you? Please step up to the window. It's your turn."

After getting the information she sought, Elizabeth turned away from the ticket window hoping that Simon had not seen her. She planned to come back to the depot during her Thanksgiving break and purchase a ticket to Milledgeville. She would write a letter to her father that afternoon announcing her plans to visit him.

The train whistle caused her to abruptly flinch as the engine seemed to appear out of nowhere blowing smoke that covered the platform and the people. She lost sight of Simon and James for a moment and flinched when the sound of the train screeched to a halt.

They reappeared, but this time there was a third man walking with them. The third man was smartly dressed in a suit with a vest and long overcoat. Elizabeth returned to her waiting carriage and asked the driver to take her back home.

Petersburg bank manager, Theodore Wright, joined Simon and James. They walked towards a waiting stagecoach.

"Risky business bringing James with you," Theodore said to Simon.

"We stayed away from everyone. There won't be any problems. James and I have a deal. No more slip-ups."

"Glad to hear that," Theodore responded. "Do you have the credit records from the store?"

Simon reached into his pocket and handed Theodore a small stack of ledger cards bound with twine that James had stolen from Frank Parks' store.

"How are the foreclosures coming?" Simon asked Theodore.

"You stick to your end of the deal, and I'll stick to mine. I told you that I would start foreclosure proceedings as soon as a payment is missed. At least now with the help of these credit records, I know whose farm will be next. It's going to take time, and there is a lot of land to be had but now is not the time to be hasty. Let's not attract attention by being greedy."

"Greed is one of my better attributes," Simon answered.

"Listen to me. We must be careful. This thing could blow up in our faces," Theodore said before stepping onto the stagecoach. Leaning out the window he warned the two men, "We will all be rich and someday lay claim to hundreds of acres as long as you and your friend here don't mess this up."

"Take care, Teddy," Simon said slapping the side of the coach, signaling for the driver to proceed.

CHAPTER 23

Robert was exhausted after returning from an all-day outing in Lincolnton. "I know it's late, but I would still like to see Elizabeth," Robert said looking in the direction of his parents.

"That's fine just don't be too late, Son," William said.

Robert tied his horse in front of Kate's boarding house and walked in the front door. He went up the stairs and knocked on the door of the room that Elizabeth had described. A voice responded from the other side of the door followed by footsteps.

Opening the door Elizabeth said, "Robert, hi!"

"I need to talk with you. Can we go out front? I prefer we talk in private."

"Sure. Give me just a moment." She pushed the door shut before returning carrying a shawl.

They walked into the yard and through the front gate of the wrought iron fence. Before Robert could speak a word, Elizabeth began, "Why haven't you told me that you broke into Simon's office?"

"Is that what Simon told you?"

"Yes, he did. He also said that Christopher was a witness."

"Elizabeth, at some point you are going to have to decide whether to believe Simon or to believe me."

Sounding frustrated Elizabeth said, "That is so true, and I have to admit that at the moment Simon seems to be winning that race."

Trust in a relationship was important to Robert. He had trusted others in the past who had disappointed him and broken his heart. There was no way he would allow that to happen again. He realized that life was not easy at times, but he seemed to be experiencing more than his share of trouble. The conversation he had rehearsed was not going the way he thought it would. Elizabeth had thrown him off with her question about the conflict at Simon's office. Her comments like cold water had cooled the fire of his affections. Still, he was determined that a relationship with Elizabeth was worth whatever the cost. He told Elizabeth everything he knew about Simon including the distribution of moonshine and evidence that placed him at the farm of a murdered man. He explained what happened at Simon's office and about finding Anna's brooch. The story was confusing, but Elizabeth was starting to put things together, and that made her nervous.

"I am growing so weary of this battle between you and Simon. Before this morning I wouldn't have believed a word you said."

Robert looked surprised, "What about this morning?"

Elizabeth confessed that she had gone to the train depot to find out the cost of a train ticket to Milledgeville. Then she told him that she had seen Simon and James together in Vienna and that she had reservations about Simon's character after seeing them together. If Simon was as good a person as she supposed he was, then why did he meet a known criminal at the train station?

"There was another man who got off the train and joined them. They seemed to be waiting on him."

"What did he look like?"

"He was tall and round. He wore an expensive suit and hat. It was hard to tell, but I think he had a mustache."

"Did he wear a monocle on his left eye?"

"I believe so, now that you mention it."

"That's Theodore Wright, the Petersburg bank manager."

"The same bank manager who turned you down for a loan?"

"The very same. He is involved with this somehow. I just need to figure it out. It shouldn't be that hard to purchase a farm. For some reason, he is working against me. I just don't know why."

Believing Simon to be an honest man was becoming more difficult. There had been signs from time to time that caused her to question his motives, but she tried to ignore them. Every time she asked Simon about previous girlfriends, he would immediately change the subject. She also wondered why his house had been decorated in a décor that normally matched a woman's style, not that of a single man. Had there been a woman living with him in the recent past?

There was also this obsession with business and the obvious dislike of Robert and other locals he had talked about in less than gracious terms. Elizabeth had not yet told Robert about her recent rejection of Simon.

"Elizabeth, please listen to me. I know you like Simon, and on the surface, he seems like a nice person. But I have enough evidence now that I am ready to report him to the sheriff. He may have bribed the local sheriff, so I asked the Parksville sheriff, who is a friend of mine, to help me sort all this out."

Robert told Elizabeth about the gold watch with Simon's initials that he found at the site of the last tobacco barn that had burned.

"What if someone had stolen it from Simon, or maybe he had actually been at the farm in the past and somehow lost his watch? I know he has visited a lot of farms in the area. Does that sound likely to you?" Elizabeth asked.

"Anything is possible I guess."

"You have to be careful," Elizabeth demanded with concern. "I know that James is a dangerous person. If he is involved in some scheme with Simon as you say, then he may decide to come after you. I have seen what he is capable of doing."

Elizabeth's concern was palpable, yet she remained skeptical about Simon's involvement in illegal activity. Robert looked at her and again felt almost breathless by her beauty and compassionate heart. This was a deeper level of attraction than he had ever felt before. For the first time, he perceived that Elizabeth might share his feelings.

She moved in close, looked up at him, and said with a smile, "This is a terribly confusing time for me. Simon seems to want to pull me away from you, but you are special to me, Robert. I love spending time with you and your family. I'm not sure where our relationship may take us if it takes us anywhere at all. But I do want you to know that I trust your judgment and character."

Robert reached out and took Elizabeth by the hand. "I will be careful. I want to thank you for believing in me and trusting me. That means more than you know. I must go now, but will see you again soon," Robert said as he released her hand and began to turn away.

"May I ask you something before you go?"

He turned back to her, "Sure."

"Have you ever been in love?"

"Well, I didn't expect that," Robert responded. "As you already know, Anna and I courted for almost two years. I knew her from school in Parksville, but we didn't start dating until later; she was four years younger than me. She came from a wealthy family, and you might say she was a little spoiled. I don't think her parents thought me worthy of her time."

"So she was a bit of a snob, not the witch you make her out to be."

"I'm sure that I have made her sound terrible, but that's because I have never been hurt so deeply by someone before."

Elizabeth brushed a strand of hair from her face.

"What did her parents say to make you think they didn't like you?"

"I remember one time Anna told me that her mother had asked her if I was mute because she had never heard me speak," Robert laughed heartily. "As you already know, I can be a little on the quiet side, especially when I am getting to know someone or when I am in an unfamiliar crowd."

"So, you loved Anna?"

"Yes, I did, at least I did at first. I didn't think about it, I mean uh, when I saw Anna being friendly with other guys, I just thought that was her personality, she was extremely outgoing and liked to be with people. I guess you could say it ran in her family. Her parents were constantly hosting parties and gatherings for friends and neighbors. Anna was pretty, so there was no shortage of guys hanging around. At first, I went to parties with her, but being around all those people just drained me. It felt more like work than fun, so it didn't seem to surprise Anna when I asked permission to stay away from large parties. As I think back on it now, that was probably my first mistake, if you can call it that. It wasn't long after that when I noticed that Anna seemed to be changing into someone I no longer knew. It's hard to explain, but something just felt different. She seemed distracted and no longer affectionate." Robert studied the ground and hesitated, seeking something in the back recesses of his mind that did not want to be found.

"That had to be difficult," Elizabeth consoled him.

"In hopes of turning things around, I decided to surprise her one night at a party her parents were hosting. The revelry of the party greeted me outside. I rode up and hitched my horse out front along with countless other wagons and carriages. Nearing the front steps, I caught a glimpse of two embracing shadows just around the side of the wrap-around porch. Entering I asked a friend if he had seen Anna. I could tell that he was surprised to see me. He quickly turned pale, almost white. He asked me what I was doing there. Almost stuttering he told me that the last time he saw her she had been in a swing on the front porch. A sick feeling hit the pit of my stomach. The swing he mentioned was near the corner of the house where I had seen the two shadows." Robert paused and took a long, deep breath.

"Take your time, don't say more than you want to say," Elizabeth encouraged. She reached out and gently put her hand on Robert's arm.

Robert gathered himself and continued, "When I walked out, Anna was sitting on the swing with a guy I had never seen before. He had his arm wrapped around her shoulder. They sat close. When she caught sight of me walking out the door, she jumped from the swing so quickly that it almost caused her friend to fall out. She asked me why I was there and introduced me to her friend Andrew. She tried to explain that she and Andy, as she called him, had just come out for some fresh air."

"What did you do?"

"I was so confused at that point that I began to question myself. Was it possible that there really had not been anyone standing at the corner of the front porch, after all? It was a really large front porch, and the distance was pretty far from the door to the corner, not to mention the darkness. My instincts were to punch this guy and tell Anna to get lost, but…" his words trailed off while he regained his composure.

"But…," Elizabeth encouraged him to continue after a long pause.

"I didn't do either one of those. Instead, I let Anna convince me to stay and enjoy the rest of the evening with her. We went back inside, and although I am not a dancer, she talked me into dancing with her."

"What about Andrew, I mean Andy?"

"That's the funny thing. I never saw him again after Anna and I went back inside. It wasn't long after that when I heard she was seen with yet another guy."

"Thank you for sharing that with me. I know it took a lot of courage for you the revisit those memories."

"Enough about me, what about you? Have you ever been in love?" Robert asked with a smile.

"You remember the story about the boy from church? As I said, we did not see much of one another after I started college and life took over. As far as love, yes, I think I did love him. We were both young. My mother said that I had a crush on him. I wasn't sure, but she may have been right. He was a handsome, kind boy. His parents had been members of our church for years, so you could say we kind of grew up together. My first recollection of him was as a little kid who liked to play outside and occasionally got into mischief at church." Elizabeth laughed out loud. Memories flooded her mind. "David and I once sneaked into the fellowship hall at church to check out the goodies that the church ladies had prepared. There were all kinds of food and baked goods that we would enjoy after worship. He could not resist sticking his finger in the top of Mrs. Butler's world-renowned coconut cake. He crammed his finger so deep that icing stuck to his knuckles, then he licked it off and stuck it in again followed by another lick." Elizabeth was giggling so hard that she was having trouble catching her breath. "They never did find out who poked the hole in the cake. Mrs. Butler was furious, but my father was able to calm her down. During his blessing for the meal, my father gave thanks for Mrs. Butler's generosity and for her cake. Before he could say Amen, Mrs. Butler ran out the door to get more icing to patch the hole, but she was too late." Elizabeth continued barely able to get the words out. She snatched breaths between every couple of words. "That cake was eaten before she returned."

"And you fell in love with this guy?" Robert asked shifting his weight.

"Well, certainly not at first. As time passed, we found ourselves together at church and other outings. I enjoyed his company, but I also had my girlfriends for company. Our youth group at church was pretty large back in those days. I do remember the first time David kissed me. We were at the home of another friend who was having a birthday party. We were all playing hide and seek. It just so happened that David and I both ran behind the same large tree trunk close to the back of our friend's property. We stood arm to arm, and when I turned from taking another peak around the tree, his face met mine, and before I knew it, we kissed. Reflecting back now, I realize it wasn't much of a kiss, yet it was memorable."

"But it didn't end there?" Robert asked.

"No! As I said, we spent a lot of time together before I started college. To truthfully answer your question, I did love him, but our priorities changed. He intended to move away to attend college in the Atlanta area, and he asked me to go to school there too. We weren't really serious; I think he just wanted us to continue to be together. It was a difficult decision for me to choose between staying in Milledgeville to help care for my mother or going away with David. I agonized over it for a few months before I gave him my answer. That was the first time in all those years that I had ever seen him cry."

"Are you still in love with David?"

"Oh no! He got married to a girl he met in Carroll County during his junior year at Bowdon College. I hear they have a child, and that David has become a doctor. They make their home in Atlanta." Elizabeth looked up into Robert's eyes after realizing that she had been looking away.

"Thank you for sharing that story with me. It seems in a way that we have had similar experiences in our past relationships, each painful in their own way," Robert said while reaching out to take Elizabeth by the hand. "So, here is the reason I stopped by to see you today. Elizabeth, I am falling in love with you."

Elizabeth squeezed his hand and looked into Robert's crystal-clear blue eyes. "Oh Robert, I am truly humbled. I don't know what to say."

"You don't have to say anything." Robert slowly began to release the hold on her hand. "I need to get back home. Rest well and think about what I said."

"I promise," was all Elizabeth said. He turned to leave. "Robert," she called out to him. "I think I'm falling in love with you too. Take care and stay out of James' way."

Robert untied and mounted his horse for the ride home. Elizabeth waved to him one final time. When she turned to walk inside, Elizabeth saw the shadowy outline of Ruth looking down from her second-story window.

CHAPTER 24

On Sunday morning, Ruth was again near the window watching Elizabeth walk through the gate on her way to church. Once Elizabeth was out of sight, she walked into town to find Simon.

"Your scheme is failing," Ruth said to Simon after arriving at his office.

"What do you mean failing?" Simon asked.

"I'm talking about your plan to discredit Robert and capture the heart of 'yon fair maiden.'"

"Either speak English or leave," Simon snapped.

Ruth told Simon what she had seen last night from her window of the boarding house.

"That's enough," Simon complained loudly. "I will take matters into my own hands. Once again you have somehow managed to disappoint me. I should have known that I was going to have to take care of Robert Chambers myself."

Ruth shouted, "You don't know the meaning of disappointment. I will bend the ear of the sheriff so badly that he won't be able to hear out of that side when I'm done, and that's just the beginning. Just wait until I finish with your friend Elizabeth. She won't be able to get another job working around children within a hundred miles of here."

Simon knew that the local sheriff would care less about any complaints brought by Ruth. His monthly cash stipend for keeping Simon out of trouble was twice what he earned as a law officer. Ruth continued to argue with Simon not realizing that the office door was not fully closed.

"Do what you want with Elizabeth. I am done with her," Simon said in an angry tone.

"Aw! The sad sound of a jilted lover almost brings me to tears," Ruth rolled her eyes at Simon.

Robert's father had ridden into town to look at Saturday's tobacco auction posting while Robert watched the ferry for him. Auction prices were posted at the end of each week showing the most recent prices paid. William had every intention of getting back into tobacco farming as soon as possible; therefore, he felt it was important to keep up with current pricing. The warehouse for tobacco and cotton were not far from one another. He paused, hearing loud voices coming from Simon's open office door not far away. He walked the short distance over to the cotton broker's office and paused a moment before he pushed slightly on the door revealing Simon and Ruth facing off with one another.

"Shut up! I have plans to take care of Elizabeth…," Simon's words were interrupted when he looked up and saw William Chambers standing in the doorway. "Mr. Chambers, how long have you been standing there?" Simon turned with a quick smile.

"Hello, Simon! How are you, Ruth? I was just looking at the tobacco posting when I heard loud voices coming from your office. Just wanted to be sure everything was all right."

"Of course," Simon replied. "My friend Ruth and I were just discussing how low those tobacco prices were yesterday. I am pretty upset about it. I apologize if we startled you."

"Oh no, you didn't startle me. I was just concerned when I heard the commotion. Well, good day then," William said turning away from the door, leaving it ajar.

"Goodbye Mr. Chambers," Ruth responded.

———

WILLIAM RODE BACK ARRIVING just as Robert was finishing breakfast. Martha and Susie were busy tidying the kitchen.

"Where were you?" Robert asked his father.

"You know I can't be a ferryman forever. I rode into town to look at yesterday's auction prices."

"How did they look?"

"The prices were at an all-time low. If our tobacco farming friends make it through this year it will be a miracle."

"Father, have you noticed the decline of tobacco farms around here? I don't see any future in tobacco."

"You're probably right, but I'm getting too old to learn new crops. How are your talks going with the bank?" William asked.

"Not good. Every time I find a new farm, the bank president finds a new reason not to let me buy it. I don't understand. Simon Hale is buying farms left and right."

"That reminds me about something I need to tell you."

"About buying a farm?"

"No! About Simon Hale. I just overheard Simon arguing with Ruth Garrett through an open door at his office. They were shouting."

"I wonder why Ruth was there?"

"I don't know, but I heard her say something about Elizabeth."

"Elizabeth," Robert snapped. "Did you hear what she said?"

"I couldn't make out all the words, but I had the feeling that Ruth is not fond of Elizabeth. I thought she said something about seeing that Elizabeth might not be able to teach anymore."

He leaned his chair away from the table holding himself steady with his hands. His pulse quickened and his temper flared. He understood why Ruth or Simon would be seeking to do harm to him, but why Elizabeth? His feelings for Elizabeth were too strong to allow her to be discredited.

Robert's voice rose to a pitch startling his family. "I have been patient and tried to turn the other cheek as the good book says while other people have sought to run me down with lies and rumors. Enough is enough. I will not let Anna, Ruth, Simon, or anyone else continue to play me for a fool."

"What are you going to do?" William asked.

"First, I'm going to protect Elizabeth from being harassed by this cast of clowns; then, on Monday morning I will see to it that I am being treated fairly by the bank."

Robert shoved his chair back from the table with such force that it fell over. Picking it up, he apologized to his mother and darted out the door. Robert mounted his horse and rode to town in search of Elizabeth. He remembered that she would be at church, so he rode to the churchyard and waited outside for the service to end. He knew that he was too angry to walk into a house of worship at that moment.

The front door of the church opened about fifteen minutes later. The pastor stood outside facing the open-door greeting members who began filing out, stopping long enough to shake his hand. Elizabeth and Kate exited together. She did not see him standing in the churchyard.

"Robert's here," Kate announced.

Robert stood holding the leash of his horse in one hand and his hat in the other. Elizabeth noticed his look of concern.

"Give me a moment," Elizabeth spoke to Kate.

She walked over to Robert, "Is something wrong? Are you okay?"

"Elizabeth, we have to talk now," he demanded.

"Robert, please calm down. You're frightening me. Wait just one second, I will be right back."

Elizabeth walked back to Kate. "If you don't mind, I

am going to walk home with Robert. I will see you back at the boarding house." Kate agreed with a smile and went on her way.

"Please tell me what's bothering you."

Robert's eyes looked cold and hard. "My father was in town to check the prices of tobacco when he accidentally overheard an argument between Simon and Ruth. They were in Simon's office, but the door was not shut."

"Why were they arguing?"

"My father couldn't say for sure, but he overheard Ruth saying something about you not being able to teach around here again."

"What! Why would she say that?"

"I wish I knew. What I can tell you is that I'm concerned about your safety."

Elizabeth asked, "What reason would either of them have to harm me?"

"I can't answer that, but one thing I know for sure, they are using you like a pawn on a chess board so that they can get to me."

"What issue do they have with you?"

"I'm a threat to them now."

Robert presented all the evidence from the loss of their own tobacco farm to the recent murder of his good friend

Frank Parks. He did not withhold any information. He also told Elizabeth about his previous relationship with Anna and about Ruth's advances.

"Oh my gosh! Not only Anna but Ruth as well?" Elizabeth was stunned. She was beginning to understand why Ruth had been acting strangely towards her.

Robert continued, "It's time to tell the sheriff everything we know. Joseph has been investigating Simon behind the scenes for several months. He needs to hear what you know about this James character."

"Are we doing the right thing? It's just"—she hesitated – "it's just that things are moving so fast. Once we get involved in this, there will be no turning back," Elizabeth said with concern.

"The way I see it, it's either them or us."

"I don't know. Can't we wait…," Elizabeth said.

Robert interrupted, "Wait for what? Until one of us is dead? We need to act now."

"Dead!" Elizabeth wrinkled her brow. "How can you say that, Robert? We are talking about small-town people. People we know and who know us. How is it that you can even think about them as being someone who would be willing to kill or even harm us?"

"I know it may sound crazy, but please, think about

what you just witnessed. You just told me that you saw Simon with a man who was once in prison for murder. I agree that I don't think that Simon or Ruth would ever be able to carry out such an act of violence, but they might ask James to do it for them."

"But I don't...," Elizabeth began when Robert interrupted.

"Elizabeth. I care about you, and I will never allow anyone to hurt you. More than that," he continued. "I need you. My life would never be the same again if I lost you, too."

Elizabeth looked up at Robert who was wiping a tear away with the sleeve of his shirt. "What do you mean by if you lost me, too? Were you referring to losing Anna?"

Robert studied the ground as if searching for words that had already been written but were too painful to re-read. When he looked up once again at Elizabeth, his chin began to quiver. Words tried to form from somewhere deep inside his soul. "Do you remember me telling you that I was the oldest child in my family?"

"Yes, I remember. What is it, Robert?"

"My parents had three children. I had an older brother. One day when I was fourteen, my brother asked if I'd like to go fishing in the river. My father gave us permission, but he told us not to stay long since it was already getting late in the afternoon. My brother had fished this part of the river most of his life."

Robert began to struggle to draw breaths. His chest rose and fell, and his head slowly moved side to side. Elizabeth moved in closer and placed her hand on his shoulder.

"We hadn't caught any fish, and it was a hot, humid day. My brother suggested that we go swimming. I knew that our mother would never allow that. She was always anxious anytime we went on a family picnic and all three of us went swimming. He jumped in first and began to swim out a way before I slowly waded in myself. We didn't even bother to take off our shirts and pants since we didn't have anything to change into anyway."

Robert paused and took deep breaths, "The current was swift that day, and I was too frightened to go in past waist-deep. I looked back at the shore to be sure I wasn't out too far. It was then that I realized that the sounds of my brother swimming in the water had been replaced by the sound of the splashing whitecaps on the surface. When I turned, he was gone."

Robert now began to visibly shake as the thoughts and memories overcame his ability to control his emotions. Elizabeth waited in silence, then she slowly wrapped her arms around Robert whose tears came flooding down his cheeks. He heaved with deep sobs of pain spilling from every pore of his body. She stood holding him as he attempted to regain control and continue.

"I called loudly to him from where I was standing, but the silence was deafening. I made my way back to the shoreline and ran as fast as I could along the bank in the direction of the flowing river. I began to panic when I realized that since we were down in a valley, darkness would set in soon. I ran so far that I was afraid that I might be lost when I saw something floating near a gravel bar at a bend in the river. By now I was running and crying out --- No! Peter, No! ---. He was lying face down in the shallow water, not moving. I grabbed his belt and pulled his body onto the shore. When I rolled him over, his eyes were closed, and his face was dark. I screamed for help at the top of my lungs knowing that I wouldn't be heard. I cried and wept aloud staring at my brother's body, not knowing what to do. It was just then I heard a dog barking. Hoping that someone lived close who could help, I ran towards the sound of the dog who never ceased his howling. Just through the trees, I could see a flicker of light coming from a small cabin. The man living in the cabin went back with me to the river, and he dragged my brother's body to a clearing in the woods. Then he got his wagon. After loading my brother's body in the bed he covered him with a sheet and drove us home."

Once again Robert hesitated and struggled to find the strength to continue. "The screams from my mother still echo in my head at night when I try to sleep. He was buried at the cemetery in Parksville."

"Oh, Robert," Elizabeth said softly. "I am so sorry."

"My mother often said that she lost two sons to the river that day. After the shock wore off, I became angry and rebellious. My anger turned inward, and I began finding myself becoming less interested in being around people, even my own family. The reality of replacing my brother as the oldest son quickly became evident the next planting season. I'm not sure how I was able to finish school."

Robert looked up at Elizabeth for the first time since he began to share the story about his brother. By now, tears were on both of their cheeks. They fully embraced one another. Robert held on to her tightly.

When they broke their embrace Elizabeth looked deeply into Robert's eyes. "I don't want to lose you either."

"Are you ready to talk with the sheriff now?" Elizabeth nodded, and Robert took her hand.

Together they walked the distance to the boarding house stopping once for Robert to pull her close once more. Gazing into each other's eyes they sensed a new resolve. Robert gently leaned in and kissed Elizabeth for the first time.

"I don't know what the future holds, but I pray you are a part of it," Robert said.

Light rain began to fall. Elizabeth snuggled in tighter with her head resting on his chest.

"My thoughts exactly."

Chapter 25

Later that afternoon, Robert and Elizabeth ferried across the river to see Sheriff Davidson in Parksville. Joseph was not in his office at the jail, so they rode toward his home. He lived as a bachelor in a modest home not far from the jail. Robert saw his horse tied out front. Joseph heard them approaching, met them at the door, and invited them to come inside. They sat at a dining table in the main room of Joseph's home.

Robert looked at his friend and confessed, "I'm not sure where to start."

"How about at the beginning," Joseph answered.

Robert and Elizabeth told him everything they knew about Simon and James.

After listening to their stories Joseph looked at Robert

then at Elizabeth, "So you think James Ridley killed Frank Parks?"

"You remember the poster we found, don't you?" Robert asked.

"Of course I do, but that could have been a coincidence. The fact that we found it on the floor would not hold up in court. We would need a lot more than that to prove that James killed Mr. Parks." Joseph stood and asked, "Would either of you like some coffee?"

"Sure," Robert answered looking at Elizabeth whose head nodded with approval.

Joseph walked over to a woodburning stove that was already hot and placed a percolating coffee pot on top after adding water from a small container.

"I was heating up the stove before you both got here to cook some bacon and eggs for my supper."

Joseph scratched his head. "Elizabeth, would you be willing to testify in court that this James Ridley is the same escaped convict that threatened you while you were in Milledgeville?"

Elizabeth paused, "Testify? Will I have to testify in court?"

Joseph answered, "It may not come to that, but if it did, I wanted you to have time to think about it. The defense attorneys used for regional murder cases are supplied by the state, and they can be tough. They will challenge your testimony in every way possible to see if they can get you to have second thoughts about what you saw or thought you saw. You say this was in a dark hospital at night?"

"Yes, but I could see him clearly by the light coming from the hallway."

"And how far were you from him in the hallway?" Joseph asked as the coffee aroma filled the room.

Elizabeth stuttered while looking down trying to remember the details of that awful night, "Well…uh…I'm sure it was him…at least I think it was. He was within twenty to thirty feet."

"That's what I'm talking about. With all due respect Elizabeth, you need to know that this could be an unpleasant experience for you."

Robert looked at Joseph and then at Elizabeth, "Joseph. I appreciate what you're doing. But we are confident about what we are telling you. I don't think either of us would be opposed to testifying if it came down to that."

Joseph stood and walked back to the stove and poured three cups of black coffee. "Okay then. I can't say much about my investigation, but I can tell you that this is bigger than I ever imagined. I believe that there are some very wealthy and influential people in Petersburg involved, and it has become a dangerous situation. For all I know, the Petersburg sheriff may be in on it too. We are all at risk now."

Robert breathed with a deep sigh and asked, "What else can we do?"

"For your own good, leave this up to me and try to stay out of it. I will be working on this tomorrow. In the meantime, keep an eye out for anything suspicious. Be careful and don't go out alone at night."

Elizabeth seemed visibly shaken by the sheriff's warning. As they walked on the front porch storm clouds gathered in the distance.

After both were seated in the wagon, Elizabeth asked, "Do you think we will have to go to court?"

"It sounds possible. Are you sure you're okay with all of this? You know that I have enough evidence to support a case against Simon and James even without your testimony."

"You're probably right. Let's just wait and see what develops and not get too far ahead of ourselves."

"That's good advice. We need to hurry straight home before we get caught in the storm. Giddy up," Robert commanded as he snapped the reins, and the wagon pulled away.

"I did bring my parasol so maybe we won't get too wet."

The rain was infrequent but a constant threat under the darkening sky. They crossed the river on the ferry along with a few passengers. Robert's father was still working that afternoon.

"You might want to hurry and get Elizabeth home, Son. I can tell that a storm is coming. The waters are not as calm as usual. I'm going to the house myself after this," William said.

Robert looked at Elizabeth, "Would you like to stay with us until the storm passes?"

She answered, "It would be best for me to get back to the boarding house. I have a lot of schoolwork to catch up on but thank you for offering."

They continued their ride from the river, through town, to the boarding house. Robert assisted Elizabeth down from the wagon and walked her to the front porch. He took Elizabeth's hand and began tracing his thumb along the back of her hand.

"Are you afraid?" he asked.

"No, not really. I realize James has a bad reputation, but I truly don't believe that he or Simon would have any reason to harm either one of us."

"I'm not disagreeing with you, but I beg you to remember what Joseph told us. If you have to go anywhere after dark, please be sure to find someone to go with you."

"You're probably right. Maybe Kate or even Ruth would be willing to help."

"No, not Ruth!" Robert said with urgency. "I don't trust Ruth."

"Robert, please. Let's not overact. I have a reasonably good relationship with Ruth right now. What harm could it possibly do by asking her to walk me to town and back? Look behind you, I can see the tavern from here. It's not that far."

"I hope you're right, but I am not comfortable with the idea of you going anywhere after dark with Ruth, or even with Simon for that matter."

Suddenly a brilliant flash of light illuminated the sky followed by a clap of thunder which rattled the boarding house windows. Concerned by the ever-darkening sky, Elizabeth warned Robert, "You better get back home before this gets any worse."

"I know you're right, but I don't want to leave you, not yet," he said. "We could sit here on the porch for a while."

"I would love that except I need to catch up on my work before Kate gets supper ready."

Robert put his arms around her waist and pulled her tightly to his chest. Elizabeth removed her bonnet. He leaned in to meet her lips, kissing her gently. Robert thought that he had never experienced anything so natural.

He felt comfortable with Elizabeth thinking that he had known and loved her all of his life. He knew at that moment that he wanted to spend the rest of his life loving her just as he did right now. He sensed that Elizabeth felt the same. Their kiss was interrupted by another loud thunderclap.

"Robert, for your own safety, you really need to go home."

"Okay, I will leave but only if you agree to have dinner with me again."

"Of course I will," she replied.

"Elizabeth, you are so beautiful, inside, and out. I will see you tomorrow."

"Yes. Now please, go in."

With that, Robert turned and sprinted in the rain across the yard and pulled himself up onto the wet wagon seat. He urged the horse toward town while tilting his hat down to keep the rain out of his face. On his way, he passed the bank and vowed to return Monday to speak with the manager. The rain continued to fall with a light steady rhythm.

Approaching the tobacco warehouse, he thought he saw a man standing on the front porch. Matthew Smith walked down the front steps moving in his direction. Even from a distance, Robert could see both pain and anger in his rain-drenched face.

"Get down," Matthew demanded. Robert came to a stop in front of the warehouse.

Robert stepped down onto the muddy street, "Matthew, what are you doing here?"

With a threatening gesture of impending confrontation, Matthew pointed at Robert and asked, "Do you remember what I told you that day you and your father came to this warehouse?"

"Is Anna okay?"

"No, Anna is not okay!" Matthew raised his voice. His lips curled tightly. "She's dead!"

Robert's mouth flew open in disbelief. He stared back at Matthew. His body stiffened. "When did this happen?"

"A couple of hours ago. I came to the warehouse to be alone then I saw you and that new schoolteacher pass through town. I figured you would be coming back soon. I was right."

"Matthew, please."

"It's too late for that," he said. His fists tightened as he stepped towards Robert.

Robert put his hand out and pushed back on Matthew's chest, "Please listen to me, Mr. Smith. I know you are angry and hurt, but this is not my fault. I have never been intimate with Anna."

"That's not what I heard," Matthew barked with raised fists.

"Please hear me out first. Thomas Wright was having an affair with Anna when we were still seeing one another."

"Thomas Wright," Matthew spoke after sucking air between his gritted teeth.

"Think about it for a minute Mr. Smith. I am sure that Thomas was around your house from time to time. Had it never occurred to you that he might have been involved with Anna?"

"Of course it did, but I was told…."

"You were told what, that I was the one to blame? Why would Thomas say that unless he was trying to hide his own misdeeds? He never liked me, so I became his scapegoat. He began spreading nasty rumors about my relationship with your daughter. Look, Mr. Smith, I loved Anna at one time, and I still care for her, but she caused me a lot of pain when I found out that she was seeing Thomas behind my back. I promise you that what I am saying is true and that Thomas has been lying to you just as he lied to Anna."

Rain dripped off the front bill of Matthew's hat. The big man lowered his head seemingly to consider Robert's words. Robert was prepared for the worst but was not prepared for what happened next. Suddenly Matthew's fists dropped, his shoulders slumped, and his whole body began to shake with deep sobs. The proud man was broken. Robert placed his hand on Matthew's shoulder while he continued to sob now louder than before, "I am so sorry, Mr. Smith. Come, let's get out of the rain." They turned together and walked back to the porch. Robert did his best to console the grieving man.

———

EARLY MONDAY MORNING, SHERIFF Joseph Davidson rode to the train station in Vienna. He stopped short of the depot a few minutes prior to the train's scheduled arrival. The train billowed smoke and the track rattled. Just then the engine came into view. After it had come to a complete stop, Joseph saw Thomas Wright exit the passenger car. His suspicions had been correct. Thomas walked to the cattle car near the caboose, opened the door, and led his horse onto the platform. Joseph dismounted and hid behind a small patch of thick pine trees and brush. After Thomas rode past, Joseph mounted his horse and began to follow him at a discrete distance.

About a mile before reaching the river, Thomas turned to the right on what looked like an abandoned logging road. Joseph, still at a distance, dismounted and slowly made his way down the old roadbed. He could see a trail of smoke coming from the stone chimney of a small tenant farmhouse. Thomas' horse was tied out front, but there was no sign of Thomas.

After tying his horse to a tree, Joseph began walking slowly and quietly among the trees and underbrush. The rain had dampened the ground muffling any sounds of breaking twigs. He crept up to the front of the house. Muffled voices of two men were coming from inside. He slipped his Remington forty-four caliber pistol from its holster and held it in his right hand as he slowly ascended the steps and quickly pushed the front door open.

"Raise your hands and keep them up where I can see them or the next visitor here will be the undertaker," Joseph shouted at Thomas and James, whose face he recognized from the wanted poster.

"What's the meaning of this?" Thomas asked with his hands reaching for the ceiling.

"You leave the questions up to me," Joseph retorted.

"Take your gun out slowly and drop it, then slide it over to me. Do it now!" Thomas hesitated but ultimately pulled his trench coat back exposing a holster and gun. His eyes remained on the sheriff. He removed his revolver, slowly placed it on the floor, and pushed it over to the sheriff. Joseph looked at James, "Do you have a weapon on you?"

"No!" James answered. He was wearing overalls and there was no evidence that he could be concealing a weapon.

"Both of you are coming with me. You're under arrest," Joseph announced. The two men still appeared to be in shock, unable to comprehend what was happening.

Joseph saw two pieces of rope in the corner of the room and instructed Thomas to use the shorter piece to tie James' hands together in front of him. "Since there are only two horses for three men, I suppose you will have to walk to the Parksville Jail," Joseph said looking at James.

"What do you mean? I ain't done nothin' wrong," James protested. "Why are you taking me to jail?"

"Shut up and do as I say," Joseph said loudly as his eyes darted from James to Thomas.

Thomas scoffed, "You're in big trouble, Sheriff."

"We'll see who's in trouble. Now tie the end of that longer rope around his waist. If you decide to try and get away, you'll be dragging him like an anchor."

Thomas did as Joseph asked but continued to grumble and make accusations about how his father and the Petersburg sheriff were going to have Joseph's head on a skewer.

They all exited the shack and walked down the path with Thomas' horse in tow until they reached Joseph's horse. Joseph tied the other end of the rope that was tied around James' waist to the saddle horn on Thomas' horse. Joseph and Thomas mounted the horses while James followed on foot.

"Pick up the pace James," Joseph said looking back at his disgruntled prisoner. "It's a long walk to Parksville from here."

The steady rain began to intensify.

Chapter 26

By noon on Monday, word of the arrests had spread across Petersburg. Theodore Wright and Petersburg Sheriff Edward Scott rode to Parksville together in Theodore's closed carriage to personally investigate the situation.

After arriving, the two men stomped their muddy feet on the front porch of the jail before entering, where they found Joseph sitting at his desk.

"Joseph," Theodore blurted. "What's the meaning of arresting my son?" Theodore was a large and intimidating man who was used to getting his way.

Joseph stood without even flinching at the booming voice of the bank manager from Petersburg, "He is being held for questioning in relation to the murder of Josh Martin."

"Josh Martin," Edward scoffed. "That poor kid died in a barn fire accident at his home."

"At least you're right about one thing! He did die," answered Joseph looking at Edward. "But I have eyewitness testimony that it was not an accident, and that Thomas was involved."

"That's preposterous," Theodore bellowed. "How much is my son's bail?"

Joseph told Theodore that the judge had set bail at five hundred dollars. Theodore withdrew ten fifty-dollar bills from a vest pocket in his overcoat and handed it to Joseph.

"Bring him out to me, now!" he demanded.

Joseph stared at both then reluctantly turned towards the locked steel door with a barred small window. The doorway led to the interior of the jail which contained separate cells.

Sheriff Scott stood to the side but intently observed. Joseph unlocked the door.

"Stand back unless you want to join them," Joseph demanded seeing Theodore's attempt to walk into the interior room along with him. The sound of a set of keys opening another cell door could be heard just before Joseph escorted Thomas to the front office. James stood in a separate cell watching through the bars.

"Hey, what about me? Don't leave me here."

Joseph looked at Theodore, then at Edward, "His bail has not been set, so he's not going anywhere for now."

Theodore spoke to James, "I'll be back for you as soon as the judge sets bail." Theodore turned to Joseph, "My lawyer will be in touch Sheriff. You had better get your facts together. You have a lot of explaining to do."

The three men stormed out the front door and into the waiting carriage. They stopped by the livery stable where Thomas retrieved his horse, mounted it, and rode away.

———

SIMON WAS WAITING FOR all three men back inside the shack. "Where's James?" he asked.

Sheriff Scott answered, "The judge did not set bail for James. Charges against him are more serious."

"Do you know the judge?" Simon asked.

"I know who he is, but I have never met him. He just moved to Parksville from Augusta. I will see what I can do."

Simon's nostrils flared and his face turned red. "How did the Parksville sheriff find James? We have been careful to keep him out of sight."

"He must have followed me here from the rail depot in Vienna," Thomas answered. "I was just returning from visiting a lady friend of mine in Columbia."

"I should have known that it would have something to do with you and your association with a woman," Simon remarked sarcastically. "We have to be more careful," Simon retorted slamming his hat down on the table. "How could you have been so blind not to notice that you were being followed? Do you have any idea how reckless you have been and how much is at stake here? If I go down because of this, then both you and your father will go down with me."

"Calm down Simon," Theodore said. "I am sure my son will be more careful from now on. Won't you, Son?"

A look of complacency answered the question.

"Thomas!" Theodore bellowed so loud it sounded like a clap of thunder.

Thomas looked at his father and without a word, turned and walked outside.

Simon and Theodore exchanged worried glances.

"Don't worry Simon, I can take care of him," Theodore responded. "For now, we need to be more concerned about James. The Parksville sheriff may attempt to get information out of him."

"James would never talk to him or anyone else in

Parksville. He may not look so smart, but he has been in and out of jail enough to know what he should and should not say," Simon said.

The tension in the room began to dissipate.

"I hope you're right, for all our sakes," Theodore said.

"Simon, what do you think we should do?" Edward asked.

"I'm not sure. One thing I do know, James knows how to break out of jail. Whatever we do, I think we need to move quickly. The longer he is in there, the more we are all at risk," Simon answered.

With that, Theodore and Sheriff Scott departed and returned to Petersburg.

—

SIMON STAYED IN THE shack that afternoon making plans to break James out of jail. Sheriff Scott had described the layout of the jail, so Simon knew where to find the cell keys. He would have to pick the right time knowing that the sheriff would be staying close by with his prisoner now behind bars. The rain pelted the tin roof of the old shack so loudly that it sounded like a passing train. Water dripped through the roof in several places. Walking out into the rain, he cursed under his breath and got on his horse. His next stop would be Parksville.

For the next two nights, Simon watched the jail from the window of an abandoned building making note of when Joseph came and went. Every evening around mealtime the sheriff went home and returned about an hour later bringing food for his prisoner. He was on the lookout again Friday night when the sheriff rode away following his familiar pattern. Simon looked in all directions, seeing no one, he quickly covered the distance to the jail. To his surprise, the front door was unlocked. His shadowy figure danced on the wall as he moved towards the desk where a small lantern glowed. He opened the bottom right drawer and found the jail cell keys just where Sheriff Scott had described.

"It took you long enough. Hurry up! I'm cold, wet, and tired of eating bread and beans every meal," James told Simon. Simon moved swiftly to unlock the cell door.

Sheriff Davidson had not ridden far when the thought occurred to him that he might not have locked the front door of his office. The knowledge of having a prisoner in custody motivated him to go back and check the door. By now the rain fell so hard on the tin roof of the jail that it drowned out all sounds making it impossible for Simon or James to hear the sheriff's return. They were both walking through the door that led to the office when Joseph opened the front door.

Startled, Joseph looked at the two men and reached for his gun. The sheriff was unable to remove his revolver fast enough to take proper aim. Simon, who was an expert gun handler, pulled his revolver first. Two shots rang out, lighting up the room briefly. Gunpowder spewed from both revolvers. Joseph's shot hit the wall immediately behind Simon and James barely missing them. Simon's shot struck Joseph in the chest sending him stumbling backwards until he struck the wall and crumpled to the floor.

"Hurry," Simon barked, "In here." They dragged the body of the sheriff into a cell and locked the door. "Let's get out of here," Simon growled while running out into the rain. James mounted the sheriff's horse, and Simon ran across the street to retrieve his own. They rode back to the shack in the pouring rain.

"Do you think anyone saw us?" James asked.

"I don't think anyone would have heard the gunshots above the sound of thunder."

"He almost shot me," James said. "We have done some bad things, but we ain't never killed a lawman before."

"Do you think for a minute that I wanted to shoot someone tonight? I thought we were in the clear when I saw him ride away. Anyway, none of this would have happened if that idiot Thomas had been more careful. I will personally snatch that silver spoon from his mouth and shove it down his throat," Simon growled. "They won't find his body until tomorrow. At daybreak, we'll cross the river and finish the job in Petersburg. We'll bed down here for tonight."

Simon knew that James was right about the shooting of a lawman. Simon had killed a distiller in Atlanta after a heated argument about a missing payment. When the man brandished a knife, Simon drew his gun and shot him twice. After the shooting, James and Simon decided that they needed to leave Atlanta. James went East to Augusta and Simon went North to Petersburg.

Simon sat in a chair looking out the window, hoping that they had not been seen or followed. James stretched out on a blanket near the fire and before long began snoring lightly. Simon was on edge hearing limbs snapping off trees and at times hitting the roof of the shack. The rain and wind created haunting sounds in the woods throughout the night. Rain blew through the cracks in the walls making the room damp. As Simon sat, his thoughts shifted to Robert Chambers. Robert, who knew too much, was becoming a real threat. He could destroy all his plans. Robert had already caused Elizabeth to question his character. Just one more reason to hate him. No one would stand in his way. Robert Chambers was next on his list of problems to eliminate.

CHAPTER 27

Early Saturday morning, rain pelted the tin roof of the old shack, as distant thunder still rumbled and occasionally rattled the building. Simon had not been able to sleep. Every time he closed his eyes, he relived the sound of gunfire and the sight of the sheriff sprawled out on the floor of the jail. His sleep was also stolen because of Robert and Elizabeth. They had seen and heard too much, which made Simon uncomfortable, assuming the stories he had been hearing from Ruth were true. He admitted to himself that he liked Elizabeth, but not even a beautiful woman like her would stop him from attaining great wealth. He woke James, who complained before he sat up and threw another log in the fireplace.

"I have a new plan," Simon said looking at James

who was standing in front of the fire. "It involves Ruth," Simon told James about how he planned to use Ruth to help them once they got back across the river.

"Can Ruth be trusted?" James asked.

"I can handle Ruth."

Realizing the recent rain might cause the river to be swollen and impassible, the two men agreed to get to Petersburg as early as possible. They hoped that it was not too late for them to cross knowing that the ferry might not operate in this condition. The shutdown of the ferry would also delay any news from crossing the river about the shooting of Sheriff Davidson.

Early the next morning at the staging area, light allowed visibility from one side of the river to the other, but the fog was moving in. From where they stood, they could see William Chambers standing on the opposite shore surveying the river from his front porch.

Simon began waving his arms frantically signaling that they wanted to cross. William looked up and saw the two men on the other side. The river had risen far above its normal boundaries and the staging areas on both sides would soon be underwater. Even though he knew better than to risk it, he decided to go ahead and cross for these two customers who appeared to be desperate.

He decided that when they returned to the Petersburg side, he was going to close the ferry until it was safe again to operate.

The crossing took twice as long as usual, and William was too busy navigating the flooded river to pay any attention to the two men he had gone to retrieve. At one point he had to stop and wait for floating debris to pass in front before continuing. The flat-bottomed vessel pitched up and down in the swift current almost knocking William off his feet and causing him to lose his grip on the pole he used to push the ferry forward. He quickly picked it up and stood upright again although not yet stable. Simon and James held tightly to the reins of their horses. Finally, the boat passed through the most violent part of the current and began pushing through water that was calmer near the landing area. William secured the ferry by tying a thick rope to a large tree on the shore while his two riders exited onto dry land.

"That was foolish of me. We shouldn't have been on the ferry in that current," William said. He thanked Simon, who paid the crossing fare. "If you see the Petersburg sheriff, please tell him that the ferry will be closed until the river calms down."

Simon nodded to acknowledge William's request

avoiding any small talk that might result in questions about his traveling partner. They mounted up and rode directly to Simon's house. Once again, rain began to fall.

"Do you think he recognized the sheriff's horse?" James asked Simon.

"I doubt it! He was too busy keeping us above water to pay any attention to our horses."

Both men dismounted in front of the house. Simon opened the front door and immediately saw Ruth Garrett sitting at the table near the stove.

"Timing is everything," Simon said while looking at Ruth.

"What are talking about?" Ruth asked. "I came over to tell you about Robert's plans to have lunch with Elizabeth today. Your front door was unlocked so I just came on in and took my normal seat. I figured you would be back soon."

"We were just talking about you," Simon continued.

"Well, by all means, let me hear what you have to say."

"We are set to make a lot of money by buying up land, but the process is slow," Simon pulled out a chair next to Ruth. James joined them after removing his wet overcoat and hat.

"Go on," Ruth encouraged raising an eyebrow. "I'm all ears."

"I have one big problem," Simon went on as his gaze turned dark and his eyes narrowed.

"Let me guess," Ruth interjected. "Robert Chambers?"

"We have to find a way to silence Robert once and for all before he ruins everything. I eliminated one threat last night at the Parksville jail. The sheriff and Robert have been spending a lot of time together. We won't have to worry about the sheriff again, but I don't know who else Robert is talking to, that is except Elizabeth of course."

"Wait, Simon, what did you just say about the sheriff in Parksville? Are you telling me that you killed a sheriff?" Ruth asked as her eyes glanced uneasily between Simon and James.

"It was an accident," James said.

Simon's lips flattened. His eyes looked as cold as a January night in North Georgia. "I didn't plan on killing anyone. Anyway, the sheriff can blame himself for that, he drew first. Besides, he would still be alive if he had not changed his routine and doubled back to the jail."

Ruth suddenly looked restless. She stood up from the table, pushing her chair back. It appeared that she was playing through scenarios in her mind about what might happen to her in the future if she continued to try and help Simon. "I can't do this," Ruth said trying to clear her throat.

Simon also stood, "What do you mean, Ruth? Until now you wanted to be a part, to be rewarded for your efforts. After all, how much can you make as a schoolteacher?"

She glared at Simon, "That was before you started killing people. "I'm going home. I don't want any part of this."

Ruth turned towards the door but was stopped cold in her tracks.

"Stop!" Simon shouted as he drew his revolver from the holster and pointed it at Ruth. His words came in a low controlled tone, "You don't have a choice anymore. You will do as I say if you intend to live to teach another day."

Staring down the barrel of a gun caused Ruth to shake uncontrollably.

"Here is how this is going to work," Simon continued forcing Ruth to sit back down at the table.

—

ELIZABETH AND KATE NORMAN had just finished breakfast and were enjoying a moment of conversation.

Kate said, "I was surely saddened by the death of Anna Smith."

"Me too," Elizabeth responded. "I am sorry that I did not attend the funeral. But I really didn't know her even though Robert mentions her at times."

Kate went on, "I saw Robert standing in the back of the sanctuary during the entire service. Anna's parents were so distraught. I felt terrible for them. Anna had been through a lot in the last months of her life."

"This will impact them for the rest of their lives. Some folks get better, and some folks get bitter from a sudden loss like this," Elizabeth said.

"You should know," Kate responded.

"Changing the subject," Elizabeth continued. "I don't know how you do it Kate, but that was some of the best sausage and pancakes I have ever eaten."

"Why thank you. It's no real secret. I'll show you sometime. What are your plans for today?"

"If the rain stops, I plan to walk to the tavern and have lunch with Robert."

"You two have been spending a lot of time together lately."

"I guess we have."

"Is this becoming serious? I would hate to lose you as a tenant."

"Robert and I are enjoying each other's company, and I have to admit that even though I wasn't planning on it, it seems that we are falling in love."

"First comes love, then comes marriage as they say," Kate said with a bright smile.

Elizabeth laughed, "It's a little early for that. Anyway, I wouldn't talk marriage with any man until he met my father."

"Well, I have said for years that Robert Chambers is one of the nicest men I have ever met. You have my approval if it turns out that he is the one."

"Thank you, Kate. I will remember that."

Kate took the dishes to the sink. Elizabeth walked upstairs to her room. She was happy that Ruth had not come down for breakfast that morning. Elizabeth was in no mood to have any discussions with her. During a brief conversation with Ruth after school on Friday, Elizabeth mentioned that she might be having lunch with Robert on Saturday. At noon she rose from her desk to join Robert and realized she had still not heard any sound coming from Ruth's room.

The sky was dark and foreboding while the winds picked up, but the rain had subsided for now. Elizabeth exited the boarding house to meet Robert. She had not walked far when she heard a voice call to her from the shadows beside a vacant building. She looked up to see Ruth Garrett motioning for her to come over.

CHAPTER 28

"Ruth, what are you doing here?" Elizabeth asked. Ruth eased back even further into the shadows and away from the street. It was just then that Elizabeth sensed they were not alone. James appeared out of nowhere from behind a tall stack of lumber. With one hand he put a finger to his lips giving a sign for Elizabeth to be quiet. In the other hand, he held a large hunting knife and a white handkerchief. James placed the handkerchief in her mouth and tied it tightly.

Ruth said, "Elizabeth, this was not my idea, please forgive me."

"Shut up or I'll put this knife at your throat next," James scoffed. "Move, both of you, now. Do as I say, and don't try to escape," James added tapping on a revolver strapped around his waist.

They all walked a few steps behind the building and climbed into Simon's wagon. The wagon seat was just wide enough for all three of them. James got in, sheathed the knife, removed the revolver from its holster, and trained it on Ruth and Elizabeth.

"One word out of either of you and I swear I'll shoot," he said.

Simon knew that it was too risky to go back to his house, so he waited for them in an abandoned cabin just outside of town. Upon arrival, James forced both women out of the wagon and into the cabin while Simon held the door open.

"Quickly, get inside," Simon said. His eyes danced between both of the women.

Elizabeth was terrified even though she tried to conceal her fear.

"Take that thing out of her mouth," Simon ordered James.

He untied the knot and pulled the handkerchief away. Elizabeth took a deep breath and tried to calm herself.

"Simon, why are you doing this?" Elizabeth asked with a shaky voice.

"I am sorry it had to end this way, Elizabeth. I was truly beginning to enjoy your company."

"Just like you enjoyed mine, huh?" Ruth said with a look of disgust on her face.

A loud pop resonated in the room as Ruth's head jerked suddenly sideways from Simon's open hand slap. Ruth let out a small groan and reached for her face. Elizabeth let out an audible gasp.

"Listen to me," Simon's voice boomed. "Both of you sit down over there on the floor, and I better not hear so much as a whisper from either of you." They both moved slowly and sat with their backs against the wall of the old cabin. Ruth began to quietly sob but Simon ignored her.

"What do we do now?" James asked looking at Simon.

"I told you that I had a plan, and we are right on schedule. We will just wait here a while longer for the rain to slow down, then we will make our way back to our place across the river."

James gave a confused look at Simon and asked, "You plan to cross the river, now, in this weather?"

"We don't have a choice. It will buy us a little more time."

"But Simon, you know what the ferryman said about closing the ferry, right?" James protested.

"We've crossed the ferry enough to know how it works. We can do it without his help."

Elizabeth hugged her knees, dropped her head, and trembled with fear.

Simon continued, "Tomorrow when the weather calms down, I will write a ransom note that you will take to Thomas, and he will deliver it to Robert. In the note I will arrange a meeting point, when he shows up, we will be waiting."

At the sound of Robert's name, Elizabeth's head turned up quickly and her eyes widened, "Simon, please, what is it that you want? Why are you doing this?"

Simon looked at Elizabeth, "I don't want to hurt you. This would have never happened if it hadn't been for that farmer-turned-detective boyfriend of yours."

"What are you going to do?" Elizabeth asked.

"You will see in time. This will all be over soon."

Elizabeth's thoughts were running wild with various scenarios. Was Simon planning on killing Robert? If Robert was a threat to Simon, and Simon thought that he knew too much, then what about her? Did Simon know how much Robert had shared with her? How far was Simon willing to go?

Robert arrived early at the tavern for lunch and was having an enjoyable conversation with Christopher when he realized that Elizabeth was late.

"It's not like Elizabeth to be late," Robert told Christopher who had just delivered a glass of tea to the table.

"Maybe I should go check on her," he continued.

Christopher answered, "Okay. But before you go, tell me once again about your family outing in Lincolnton."

For the second time, Robert told his friend how much he and his family had enjoyed time away from Petersburg. They all agreed that Lincolnton seemed to be a wonderful place to live and raise a family. Robert had noticed the new textile mill in town and told Christopher that there were job opportunities other than farming.

"I'm going to walk to the boarding house and check on Elizabeth," Robert told Christopher.

"Stay dry," Christopher replied.

"Robert," he turned at the sound of Christopher's voice.

"Sorry to hear about Anna."

"Thanks," was all Robert could say.

Robert left his horse tied in front of the tavern and walked down the muddy street hoping to find Elizabeth. The rain that had once subsided now began to fall again in a slow steady pattern. He stepped onto the front porch of the boarding house and removed his rain-soaked overcoat and hat. He placed both across one of the rocking chairs and knocked on the door before to entering. The upstairs where Elizabeth and Ruth lived appeared dark, so he walked down the hall in the direction of the kitchen and Kate Norman's room. He found Kate in the kitchen putting away freshly washed plates and utensils.

"Robert, hello! I didn't hear you come in," Kate sounded surprised.

"Hello, Mrs. Norman. I hope I didn't startle you. I knocked but came on in when no one answered."

"That's just fine," Kate replied. "How can I help you?"

"I was looking for Elizabeth. She was supposed to meet me at the tavern today for lunch."

"The two of us had breakfast together this morning. She told me about your lunch date before she went upstairs to work for a while. I'm quite sure it was she that I heard leaving not long ago. Did you not pass her on the way?"

"No, I didn't. It's not like her to be late."

Kate replied, "Would you like me to help look for her?"

"Thanks, but you don't need to get out in this weather. I'm sure it's nothing to get all worked up about. Just tell her I was here when she returns."

"I will. I do remember her saying something about getting a dress made for her trip to Milledgeville. She is excited about seeing her father in a few weeks. You might stop by the home of Amelia Thornton. She may have been delayed trying on her new dress."

"Thank you, Mrs. Norman. If you see her first, please let her know where I am headed. From there I will return to the tavern to wait for her."

"Please call me Kate. By the way, I saw you at the back of the church for Anna's funeral. I am not fully aware of your relationship with her, but you were obviously in pain. I am terribly sorry."

"Thank you, Mrs. Norman, I mean, Kate."

Robert put his overcoat and hat back on and walked in the rain towards the home of Amelia Thornton, whom he had known for many years. Amelia was a retired schoolteacher who moved from Parksville to Petersburg some time ago. It would be a pleasure to see her again.

Petersburg was the kind of small town that could be traversed from one end to the other in a few minutes. Most of the homes in the area were situated just a short distance from town in either one of two directions. Robert knew that Mrs. Thornton lived on the west side of town, which was the side that was the furthest from the river. He was within a few houses of the dressmaker when a dreadful thought crossed his mind. He wondered if Elizabeth might have stopped to see Simon. She told Robert that she intended to call off their relationship. He looked back over his shoulder to the east and noticed smoke coming from the chimney of what he thought to be Simon's home just before he walked onto the dressmaker's porch.

Chapter 29

Robert confirmed that Mrs. Thornton was working on a new dress for Elizabeth, but she had not seen her in the last few days. After visiting Mrs. Thornton, he said goodbye and decided to stop by Simon's house on his way back to the tavern. When no one answered the door, he gently pushed on the door but found it locked. The door around the back was also locked. He noticed large footprints in the mud out front, but in the back, there was a set of smaller prints. He understood why Elizabeth might visit Simon's front door, but it did not make sense for her footprints to be found behind the house.

Although the rain fell in torrents, he returned to the tavern to see if Elizabeth had been there. Christopher confirmed that he had not seen Elizabeth.

Robert said, "Please let her know I have been in twice looking for her."

"Sure thing," Christopher said. "It's slow here today. Let me know if I can help you search for her. The owner won't mind if I close down for a while."

"Thanks, Christopher. If she does come in, tell her I went home to wait for a break in the weather. I just can't understand what happened and why she didn't show up."

Christopher asked, "Do you think something bad has happened to her?"

"I'm not sure. I don't trust anyone in this town anymore, except you of course."

"If she comes in, I will ask her to stay here long enough for me to ride out and get you."

"Thanks again, Buddy."

"Be careful Robert. I don't know why, but I have a bad feeling about this. I'm keeping my rifle nearby until you get all this sorted out."

About mid-afternoon, William Chambers heard Robert knocking mud off his feet on the front porch just before the door opened.

"Come in, Son. Sit by the fire there and warm yourself up."

"Thanks, Father."

"You're soaking wet. Where've you been?"

Robert recounted the story of his plans to meet Elizabeth for lunch and his search for her.

"Have you closed the ferry?" Robert asked.

"Yes, I have. I sent word with the only two passengers I had this mornin' to tell the sheriff that the ferry would be closed until the river calms. I didn't need to ferry them two, but the way they were calling and waving their arms at me, I did it anyway."

"Did you know them?"

"One of them was Simon Hale. I couldn't place the other man. He kept his hat pulled down to shield his face from the rain. The odd thing is, I thought I recognized the horse the stranger was riding."

"What do you mean?"

"Well, the sheriff from Parksville rides a horse that looks just like the one he was on. It even looked like the same saddle."

Robert began to feel uncomfortable. Why would Simon have been so desperate to cross the river that morning, and could James have been riding along with him? How did any of this fit in with the disappearance of Elizabeth?

Robert jumped to his feet and turned towards the door. "Where are you going now?" William asked.

"I have a bad feeling about your two customers this

morning. I'm going back to town and check again with Christopher at the tavern."

"Let me come with you," William offered.

"It'd be best for you to stay here. I need to check this out on my own."

Robert walked out again into the rain, mounted his horse, and urgently rode back to town. He stopped first at the tavern to speak with Christopher only to learn that Elizabeth had not been there.

"I'm going back to Simon's house."

"How 'bout I lock up and go with you?" Christopher asked with concern.

He reached behind the bar for his rifle, and the two men walked out the front door. Once again, Robert walked up to the front door, knocked, and pushed on the door. Just like before, no one answered. Then they both walked around to the back. Most of the footprints in the mud were now either erased by the rain or filled with water to the point that they were unrecognizable. It was Christopher who first noticed a set of ruts made by a carriage or wagon that trailed away from the house to the east. They followed the ruts which led out of town. In the distance, they could see an abandoned home place. The fog was settling and the late afternoon skyline began to turn dark. None of the sun's rays were able to penetrate the heavy, wet clouds. A small stream of smoke rose from the chimney, but it was hard to tell where the fog began, and the smoke ended.

Robert pointed in the direction of the old house, "I see a wagon around back."

They walked slower so as not to attract any attention. Christopher raised his rifle when they were less than fifty yards from the side of the house. Suddenly, two shots rang out from a partially opened window. The first bullet buzzed by Robert's head striking a tree behind him. The second shot struck Christopher's ear causing him to drop the rifle. He reached for his wound. Instinctively, Robert grabbed Christopher's free arm and quickly pulled him to the ground behind a nearby tree leaving the rifle lying in the mud a short distance away.

"You okay?" Robert looked intently at Christopher not yet knowing the extent of his wound.

"It just nicked me. I'm fine," Christopher answered. Just then two more shots spewed fire from the window of the old house.

They both stretched out face down in the mud. Christopher continued to dab his ear wiping away blood that was trickling down his cheek to his chin. Robert looked up and saw several people run from the house and get into the wagon. Christopher stood to run towards his rifle. Another shot cut in their direction and again Robert pulled him back down. They watched the wagon quickly pull away.

"We have to get to our horses," Robert said retrieving the rifle and handing it to Christopher. They ran back to the tavern.

Robert's horse was still tied out front. "You go ahead," Christopher shouted. I will get my horse and meet you."

Robert delayed for a moment thinking that he should not leave his wounded friend behind. "Hurry," Christopher demanded. "It looks like they are headed towards the river."

Chapter 30

Robert untied his horse from the hitching post, quickly mounted it, and rode hard and fast towards the river. It was then he realized that he did not have a gun or any other type of weapon. He had seen two men and two women in the fleeing wagon. He recognized Elizabeth struggling to pull free from the grip of a man he assumed to be James. He thought to himself that it must have been Simon who fired the shots at them. With his horse now running at full speed, the rain pelted his face making it difficult to see the road. He could see the wagon tracks, but the wagon was still so far ahead that it was not yet in sight.

William Chambers heard the wagon rumbling and splashing down the road, so he walked out onto the front porch. Through the rain and light fog, he saw the figures of four people exit the wagon and move towards the ferry. He called out, "Hey, what are you doing? The ferry is closed."

One of the two ladies looked in his direction for a moment, but it appeared that no one else either heard or cared what he said.

"Get on! Now!" Simon demanded while waving his revolver at the group. James was still holding Elizabeth's arm in a hammer-like grip. Her body continued to thrash in a futile attempt to pull free.

"I'm staying here," Ruth screamed stepping away from the ferry.

"Ruth, I'm warning you, get on now or else," Simon shouted back at her.

"No!" She cried back looking at the other three and then to the white-capped river. "I can't swim."

"Do as you please," Simon shouted back as another shot rang out from his revolver with a deafening boom. In desperate horror, Elizabeth looked over her shoulder and saw Ruth lying on the ground.

The situation was spiraling out of control, and Simon became unpredictable. They untied the rope that tethered the ferry to the shore. Simon grabbed the long pole used to push the ferry and applied pressure by pushing one end of the pole into the muddy bottom. It was slow at first, but the ferry finally began moving away from the bank.

"Grab the other pole and push," Simon shouted at James. The two of them pushed hard until they knew that the ferry was too far from the shore for Elizabeth to try and escape. Fortunately, Ruth had only suffered a flesh wound, and she was now making her way to Robert's house. Robert reached the edge of the river, and his body froze. He looked out across the water. Memories haunted him from a similar day years ago when he lost his brother. His legs felt like they didn't want to move. Just then he heard Elizabeth's scream shaking him from his trance.

Simon and James were so preoccupied that neither of them had seen Robert enter the water behind them. He began to swim towards the nearest end of the ferry that had already reached the main current. Floating limbs and sticks were beating against his shoulders and legs as they raced downriver in the swift current. Robert's head bobbed up and down in the churning torrent taking him under several times. All three aboard the ferry were being thrown back and forth out of control. The constant pounding of the waves splashed up and over the sides of the large flat-bottom platform. Robert reached the edge of the ferry and held on tightly trying to avoid the metal edging that lunged up and down striking the water with violent percussive-like movements. Simon was still using the long pole to keep the barge moving across the river while the waves crashed against it. A violent wave knocked James and Elizabeth off their feet. James dropped the pole, got back on his feet, and tried to walk in the direction of Elizabeth. Robert's grip on the vessel was failing from the strain. With one final effort, he forced himself up getting his upper body onto the back of the ferry, then slowly eased himself out of the water still undetected.

It was too risky for him to stand upright. The floating barge pitched and twisted in the flow. He began crawling towards the end where the others were struggling to stay on board.

"Robert!" Elizabeth screamed. Robert drew near after retrieving the pole that James had dropped.

"Stay down!" Robert swung the pole, striking James in the back knocking him overboard. His arms thrashed at the surface as his body was quickly carried downriver and out of sight. Simon pulled his revolver from the holster and pointed it at Robert, but before he could fire a shot, Elizabeth struck Simon's outstretched arm dislodging the gun and almost causing them both to fall overboard.

Robert saw his opportunity and lunged at Simon. Both men tumbled to the hard wooden floor of the ferry. Simon landed the first punch to the side of Robert's head. They struggled to stand and steady themselves. Robert ran headfirst, leading with a shoulder, hitting Simon's midsection which once again took them both to the deck. When they were able to get back on their feet, Simon pulled a knife from its sheath that had been hidden under his overcoat. Robert grabbed Simon's arm holding the knife in an attempt to keep it away from him. Just then, a floating log struck the side of the ferry with such force that it knocked all three of them down again. Simon rolled on top of Robert and sat up holding the knife over his head ready to strike when a shot rang out. Blood began to flow down the front of his vest. Simon looked up in shock to see Elizabeth holding his pistol. He dropped the knife and slumped to one side causing him to fall into the chilly water. Elizabeth was dismayed because the revolver never fired. Simon had already used all six cartridges. She looked back to the shore and saw Christopher standing with a raised rifle in his hands. Robert and Elizabeth quickly grabbed both wooden poles and in unison began pushing the ferry back in the direction of the shoreline from which they had come.

It was safer for them now that James and Simon were no longer a threat, but the river posed a bigger threat. They swayed out of control as waves and floating logs continued to pummel the sides of the ferry. In order to use the poles, it required them to stand dangerously near the edge of the platform. Elizabeth screamed. Robert turned to watch in horror as she fell into the frigid waters. He crawled quickly to the edge, grabbed her arms, and pulled her onto the platform. He handed her the pole that fortunately had not gone in the water with Elizabeth, and once again they began pushing, forcing the ferry towards the shore. After a few minutes, they had moved away from the swift flow into a calmer portion of the river where the work was not as difficult.

"Robert, are you okay?" William asked rushing to help them.

"We're fine," he said breathlessly looking at Elizabeth who strained to fill her lungs with each breath.

"Nice shot," Robert said to Christopher who had also come to their aid. "How's the ear?"

"It's fine. I was able to stop the bleeding and bandage it myself."

"Come on, let's get inside where it's warm and dry," William encouraged.

"Where's Ruth?" Elizabeth asked.

William answered, "She's inside. Martha was able to dress her wound. She is a lucky woman."

After removing some wet outer clothing, they all went into the ferryman's cottage and sat near the fire. Elizabeth was still shivering either from the cold or the realization of all that had just taken place. Martha Chambers wrapped a large wool blanket around her shoulders.

"Thank you," Elizabeth said looking up at Martha.

William asked, "Robert, what happened? You could've been killed!"

Christopher described the events that had preceded this final conflict on the river. William, Martha, and Susie listened to Robert and Elizabeth who described the kidnapping and search before the final race to the river.

"But why would they kidnap Elizabeth?" William asked.

"It's a long story. My friend Joseph can explain it all the next time we see him." Robert responded unaware that Simon had shot his friend and left him to die.

"We're glad you're okay," William said.

Robert and Elizabeth sat next to one another warming themselves by the fire. They exchanged glances and their frowns turned to smiles.

Robert looked up at his mother and saw pain etched across her brow. "Mom," was all he said. He stood, dropped the blanket, and went over and reached around his mother with both arms holding her tightly. There were no words that needed to be spoken. Several minutes seemed to pass when Martha looked up into the tear-filled eyes of her son, "That's enough now. Look, you have gotten me all wet." With that, they both laughed. "You sit while I heat up something to eat."

Martha and Susie moved to the kitchen where they stoked the fire in the stove and prepared some food.

For years now Robert had played the hand that life had dealt him, feeling that life was controlling him as opposed to him controlling his life. Looking back, it all seemed to start that dreadful day by the river when he lost his brother. Until now, he had been a compliant person, seeking to please others even at his own expense. Being more assertive felt good. The realization hit him that today he had overcome fear in a way that he had never experienced before.

"That took a lot of courage," Christopher said looking at Robert.

Robert glanced at Elizabeth, "It was worth it, and I would gladly do it again." He took Elizabeth's hand and wrapped his other arm around her shoulder. Watching from the kitchen, Susie giggled, which brought a smile to Martha's face.

Chapter 31

The train gently pulled away from the platform in Vienna. Robert and Elizabeth sat close in the first passenger car. They leaned forward looking out the window at William, Martha, Susie, and Christopher who were waving to them just before steam from the locomotive surrounded their figures, and they were no longer visible. The ride to Milledgeville would take several hours. It was Thanksgiving weekend, and they had much to be thankful for. Robert reached for Elizabeth's hand once again admiring the ring he purchased the day she accepted his proposal for marriage. It was hard to believe that a month had passed since the incident on the ferry. Now they were on their way to introduce Robert to Elizabeth's father. Elizabeth wore her new dress for the occasion.

"How would your father feel if we asked him to marry us while we are with him?" Robert asked.

"That's a bit sudden, but I am sure he would be honored if that is your desire," Elizabeth responded without hesitation.

"I didn't tell you, but I asked my parent's permission this morning, and they gave us their blessing. I was just waiting for the right moment," Robert said looking into Elizabeth's brown eyes.

"Well, I guess that settles it," Elizabeth responded.

Robert leaned in and kissed Elizabeth deeply, "I love you."

"I love you too."

Captivated by each other the ride to Milledgeville seemed short. Elizabeth's father met them at the depot. Upon seeing him Elizabeth rushed into his arms and held on tight. Recent events caused her to be more emotional than usual. After releasing her hold, she turned to Robert who waited patiently, "Father, this is Robert."

Martin Bright reached out taking both of Robert's hands. "I am so glad to finally meet you. I would say that my daughter's letters have been perfectly accurate in her descriptions of you."

"It's a pleasure to meet you, Mr. Bright."

"Please call me Martin."

"Father, we have a question."

"Wait!" Robert said looking at Elizabeth and then at her father. "Excuse me for interrupting. Before we get to that, I would like to officially ask for your daughter's hand in marriage."

"Beth and Robert, this is wonderful news. Yes! Of course. You have my blessing."

"Will you marry us?" Elizabeth asked shyly.

"It would be my pleasure."

"Now?" she asked.

"Now?" Martin asked, surprisingly.

"Well, not immediately. Just meaning while we are here." Elizabeth said.

"That is a bit sudden, but if that is what you want then, yes. We can have an informal service following worship on Sunday." Elizabeth had always wanted a small, intimate wedding. She was happier than ever and pleased to see her father doing so well. They spent the next hour talking about their plans, hopes, and dreams for the future.

After the wedding, they returned to the train station. Elizabeth exhorted her father to come with them.

"I would love nothing better, but my ministry is not finished here yet. Give me a few years, and we can talk about it again."

"Is that a commitment to retire?" Elizabeth asked.

"I pity you, Robert," Martin said looking at him with a smile. "Elizabeth could persuade a fisherman to give up fishing." Martin looked back at Elizabeth raising his eyebrows, "We shall see."

Martin and Elizabeth said goodbye once again at the train depot. This departure was less tearful than the first. On the ride home, Robert and Elizabeth talked more about the possibility of relocating to Lincolnton. There were far too many ghosts in Petersburg for their comfort, and Lincolnton was a growing community with abundant opportunity. There were multiple schoolhouses in the area where she might be able to teach. However, Elizabeth was uncomfortable with the idea of leaving her job before the end of the school year, especially knowing that it would be months before Ruth fully recovered from her gunshot wound and returned to school. William and Martha also favored the idea of moving to Lincolnton in the summer. It would be the fresh start that they all needed.

———

Summer finally arrived, and the Chambers family began loading their household goods and belongings in wagons. The plan had come together, and they were all excited. It only took one last glance over their shoulders as they stopped on the outskirts of Petersburg and looked back.

"Do you think I will turn into a pillar of salt if I take one last look?" Martha joked.

"Go ahead, hon.' I think you will be fine," William answered.

They laughed while the two wagons, loaded with all their belongings, moved westward towards the main roadway that led to Lincolnton. The early morning sun warmed their backs causing their shadows to lean in the direction of their newest hopes and dreams.

BIBLIOGRAPHY

Luking, Steve, *Last Ride On Chamberlain's Ferry*, Reidsville, NC, Melfor Publishing, 2012.

Moss, Dwain, *Ferrying the Rivers of Lincoln County*, Lincolnton, GA, *The Lincoln Journal*, September 08, 2011.

Coulter, Ellis Merton, *Old Petersburg and the Broad River Valley of Georgia*, Doraville, GA, University of Georgia Press, 1965

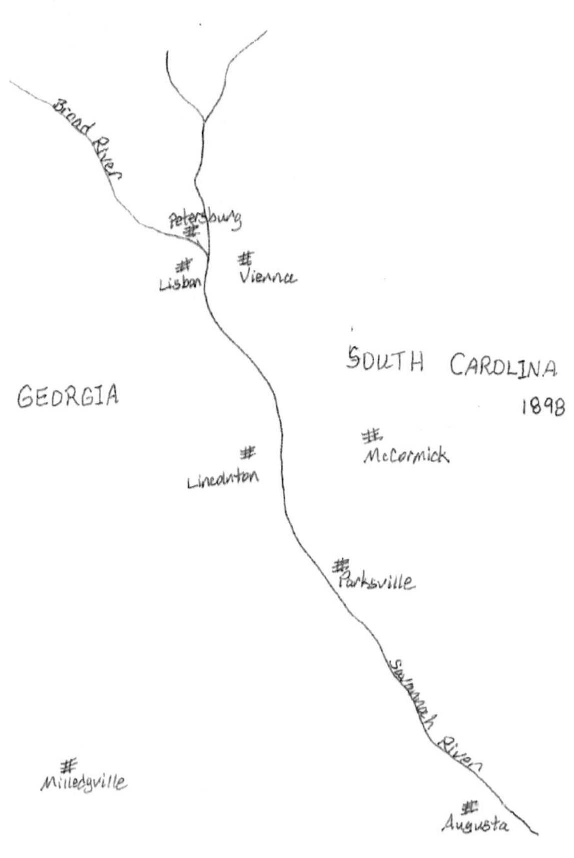

Broad River
Petersburg
Lisbon
Vienna
SOUTH CAROLINA
1898
GEORGIA
McCormick
Lincolnton
Parksville
Savannah River
Milledgville
Augusta

AUTHOR BIO

HAROLD DAWKINS LIVES IN Fayetteville, Tennessee with his wife Lee Ann. He retired after 41 years in logistics and transportation. Following retirement, Harold had the privilege of serving as a volunteer Hospice Chaplain and as Lay Pastor of his local church. He is a graduate of Jacksonville University in Jacksonville, Florida.

www.ingramcontent.com/pod-product-compliance
Lightning Source LLC
Chambersburg PA
CBHW020920110726

47900CB00001B/235